Act of Fear

A Dan Fortune Mystery

Michael Collins

OVERLOOK DUCKWORTH
New York · London

This edition published in the United States and the United Kingdom in 2013 by
Overlook Duckworth, Peter Mayer Publishers Inc.

NEW YORK:
141 Wooster Street
New York, NY 10012
www.overlookpress.com
For bulk and special sales, please contact sales@overlookny.com,
or write us at the above address.

LONDON:
30 Calvin Street
London E1 6NW
www.ducknet.co.uk
info@duckworth-publishers.co.uk
For bulk and special sales, please contact sales@duckworth-publishers.co.uk,
or write us at the above address.

This is a work of fiction. Names, characters, places, and incidents either are
the product of the author's imagination or are used fictitiously. Any resemblance to
actual persons, living or dead, businesses, companies, events, or locales is entirely
coincidental.

Cataloging-in-Publication Data is avaliable from the Library of Congress
A catalogue record for this book is available from the British Library

Printed in the United States of America

ISBN: 978-1-4683-0726-9 US
ISBN: 978-0-7156-4726-4 UK

2 4 6 8 10 9 7 5 3 1

To Hal and Anne

CHAPTER 1

It began with the mugging of the cop.

Person or persons unknown jumped the patrolman in broad daylight on Water Street near the river, dragged him into an alley, and cleaned him out. No witnesses. This is the lower west side, the Chelsea district, where alley windows are boarded up and people do not see what they're not sure they should see.

We all knew the cop: Patrolman Stettin. He's a young cop, Stettin, not long on the force and still eager. We all heard that he felt so bad about being taken that he offered to quit. That shows how young he is. Sooner or later everyone is taken in this world. This time the mugger took it all: billy club, pistol, cuffs, summons book, watch, billfold, tie clip, shoes, and loose change. The mugger was good. Stettin never even saw a shadow, according to the report I heard.

'What's a harness bull got worth stealing?' Joe Harris said.

'The pistol,' I said.

Joe Harris is my oldest friend. He never left Chelsea, the way I did over the years, but we always kept in touch. Next to Marty, my woman, Joe is my best friend. Since I've been back in Chelsea this time, we see each other a lot. Joe is a bartender by trade. Which is probably why we see each other so much. Now Joe poured me a second free shot of good Irish whiskey while he thought about Stettin's pistol.

We were in Packy's Pub, where Joe was working that day. The boss, Packy Wilson, was too busy talking to his other twilight customers about Officer Stettin to notice the free drink. We had all heard about Stettin, even though they had it under wraps. The police were annoyed. When they are annoyed they go about their work with a grim efficiency. The police did not want publicity for a mugging of one of their men, but everyone in the know had heard.

In many ways New York is a strange city. One of the ways is that in any given neighbourhood, like Chelsea or Yorkville, there are two kinds of people. There are the people who were born in, say, Chelsea, who have always lived there and most of whom always will unless they are in jail or on the run, who are part of Chelsea the way a Greek villager is part of his isolated village. And there are the people born somewhere else—maybe Queens and maybe Omaha—and who think of themselves as living in New York, not in Chelsea, people who happened to find an apartment in a section most of them don't even know is called Chelsea. Like a summer resort—the natives and the visitors. When you're a native you hear the news. I was born in Chelsea, so I rate as a native. I also rate as something else.

'No,' Joe said at last, 'there's easier ways to get a gun, Dan. Even a private snooper oughta know that much.'

Daniel Fortune, *Confidential Investigator: Reliable . . . Low Rates*. The Fortune was once Fortunowski, and there used to be a *T* in the middle for Tadeusz. That was the name my grandfather carried off the boat: Tadeusz Jan Fortunowski. When I was a boy the old men told me that my grandfather carried that name with pride, even with arrogance. Like most middle and eastern Europeans, his pedigree was a chaos of history. He was born in Lithuania, under a Russian government, of Polish parents who spoke German. But he was proud that he was a Pole, and the name was all he had to prove what he was. My father was born here. Chelsea was a world of Americans and Irish then, and a man needs to belong. My father became *Fortune.* The old men told me that my grandfather had refused to speak to anyone named Fortune, son or no son. The old man died before I was born. I never knew him. Not that I knew my father. He gave me the name—changed—and not much else. Dan Fortune, who dropped even the *T*, and who doesn't really belong anywhere. And, at the moment, a confidential investigator.

Not that I investigate much that is big or dangerous. Some industrial work and some divorces. Armed-guard jobs, and subpoenas for bread and butter. But mostly the personal problems of small people who want to apply a little pressure on someone but don't want the police. It's not work I especially like, but a man must eat, and it's work I know how to do. (Most men work at what they happened to learn how to do, not at what they wish they had learned how to do.) I'm my own boss, and I don't have to wear a white shirt or get up early. The work has one big drawback as far as Chelsea is concerned—it makes me a cop. In Chelsea that means something. It means that the only real friends I have are my woman Marty and Joe Harris. And even Joe doesn't tell me all.

'Who mugs The Man in broad daylight just for a gun?' Joe said.

Joe was right, of course. To get a handgun isn't exactly as easy as picking fruit off a tree in this country, not even in Chelsea, but there are a hundred easier ways than mugging a cop. No, Stettin's mugging was all wrong.

'Maybe just a fast buck?' I said.

'Come on, Pirate,' Joe said. 'Not even the new breed of punk strong-arms a cop for his loose change.'

'Pirate' Joe still calls me sometimes. The old nicknames stick even when a man has been away from his past as much as I have. I must know ten girls who are now six feet tall, fat, or forty, but who are still called 'Bunny' or 'Puppy'. Danny the Pirate. That was the name I got a long time ago when I lost my arm. I tell a lot of stories about how I lost the arm. Exciting stories if you buy me a beer. It's the left arm. I'm right-handed. There is some good in everything if you look at it right.

The truth is that I lost the arm when Joe and I were looting a ship. We were seventeen then. It was a dark night, and I fell into a hold. The arm broke in so many places they had to take it off just below the shoulder. Maybe if I had been rich I'd still have two arms. The city hospital didn't have the doctors or the time to take a chance on my life. That doesn't make me bitter. They saved my life. Fifty years earlier there wouldn't have been a hospital for me to be saved in. Everything is relative.

I got the loot out a porthole, and Joe dragged me off the pier and got help. The only charge the company could have made was trespassing. They made no charge. You see, my father was once a New York cop. I had friends on the force. Or, to be accurate, my mother had friends on the force. She had a lot of friends.

The cops forgot the robbery. I've got no record. The natives did not forget. It wasn't our only robbery in those days, just the one we were almost caught at. The neighbourhood knew it all. I lost my arm. The rest was inevitable: Danny the Pirate. They remember that in Chelsea. That's fine with me. It takes off some of the cop-taint. It makes the natives sometimes overlook the fact that I've lived away so much, that I say things that show I've read books. It gets me friends I need on occasion. The natives remember the seventeen-year-old pirate, and the police forget. I like it both ways.

'A cop gets killed, that figures,' Packy Wilson said to the bar in general. 'It's the robbin' and not killin' that's wrong.'

'A junkie maybe,' Joe suggested. 'He could sell the gun for a fix. Maybe use it for a show of power.'

'Could be,' Packy said. 'For a fix a junkie tries anything.'

'A junkie trembles when he sees a cop on a movie screen,' I said. 'Never a junkie.'

I could not see an addict attacking a policeman in uniform on his own beat in broad daylight. But then I did not see anyone attacking a cop under those conditions.

About then the night regulars began to come into the bar, and Packy had a cash register to mother. Joe had to begin to work in earnest. First things come first in Chelsea, as they do in the rest of the world for that matter, and there was money to be made.

Packy ended the discussion with a pronouncement. 'A cop hater. Some alley-crawler psycho with a grudge on cops.'

After that the regular customers kicked it around for a time. They did not really care about Stettin, any more than the millions who would read about Stettin in the newspapers would care, but a man has to talk about something while he drinks himself peaceful.

For a few more days it was good for a lot of talk around Chelsea and the Village. Then the talk faded. People are strange. Cops are killed in the world somewhere almost every day. A cop does not get mugged in broad daylight very often. Yet a cop killing is headlines for months, and a mugging, hot news at first, fades fast. People are more interested in death.

I might have forgotten Stettin myself in a week. I had my own troubles. Marty was getting a big play from a well-heeled customer at her club; three subpoena victims were playing a hard hide-and-seek with me; and it was too hot in the city. There was no reason to connect the second robbery and the two killings to Stettin. We get forty burglaries a day on the West Side and as many assorted crimes of violence. After a time you hardly notice the small crimes. No, a man worries about the troubles he has on hand; anything else is insanity.

So Patrolman Stettin was no more to me than good gossip. Until the kid walked into my office.

CHAPTER 2

'He's in trouble, Mr Fortune. I know it,' the kid said.

It was a Monday five days after Stettin was mugged. My office is one room on Twenty-Eighth Street. I have one window with a view of a brick wall that has turned black with the grime of the city. The window itself is dirty, so I don't have to look at the wall outside unless it is too hot. It was too hot, so I had been studying the shades of black on that wall while I waited until it was safe to call Marty and suggest a drink in a cool tavern. Since it was only eleven o'clock in the morning, Marty would not be up for breakfast for at least an hour. Marty snarls when you wake her up early. So I let the boy sit down.

'He's run out,' the boy said. 'I mean, I ain't seen him.'

'Start with the name,' I said. The boy was nervous.

'Jo-Jo Olsen,' the kid said. 'Joseph Olsen, only we always calls him Jo-Jo. I looked all week-end. No one seen him.'

'I know you,' I said. 'Pete Vitanza, right? Tony's boy?'

'Yeh,' Pete Vitanza said. 'Jo-Jo, he's my friend, Mr Fortune.'

'All right,' I said. 'He's missing how long?'

'Four days.'

I said, 'For God's sake, kid, four days isn't . . .'

'The whole week-end,' Vitanza said. 'Since maybe early Friday. We had plans like for the whole week-end. Big plans.'

'Go to the police,' I said.

Missing persons are for the police. They have the tools. Rabbits are people who have found the world too heavy. One way or another they have been pounded too hard for too long. To be a rabbit is to want to run away more than anything else on earth, and I don't like the role of the hound. That's for the police.

'Jo-Jo wouldn't never stay away right now on his own,' Pete insisted. 'He just got a new bike, a beauty. We been workin' on the motor for months. We was gonna race it Sunday. I mean, yesterday we was to race it out by East Hampton.'

'He never showed?'

'Not since Friday. He . . . was worried like. Some trouble.'

'Is he married?' Ninety-nine out of a hundred rabbits are married. Male or female rabbits. It makes you wonder.

'Hell, no. I mean, he got girls, sure. No real steady, not even the Driscoll piece. Jo-Jo and me we got motors, see? Jo-Jo he studies hard by Automotive Institute. We're gonna go over'n work for Ferrari someday.'

'He lives with his family?'

'They told me he went on a trip. I know that ain't true. He didn't take his bike. Not on his own he don't go nowhere!'

'What did he do, Pete?' I said. 'What did he pull?'

'Nothin'! I swear.'

He was nervous. He had something more on his mind.

'Come on,' I said.

He was a thin kid, tall, and he had the hard muscles all the kids have around the docks. But he was lean and scrawny. I guessed he had never eaten too well or had much of anything. His Adam's apple did a dance in his throat.

'That cop,' he said. He looked at me. 'The fuzz got beat? He got it the day before Jo-Jo faded.'

'Stettin?' I said. 'So what?'

'The bull got it right down the block from Schmidt's.'

'The garage on Water Street?'

'Yeh.'

He seemed to think he had painted a picture of great clarity. Maybe he had.

'You mean that you and Jo-Jo were doing your work on the motorbike at Schmidt's Garage?'

'Yeh. Jo-Jo he works by Schmidt's. I mean, he works there regular, 'n the last couple months we been workin' on the new bike there.'

What Pete Vitanza was trying to tell me, in the inarticulate manner of Chelsea, was this: Jo-Jo Olsen was missing when he had no reason to be missing that Pete knew, and every reason to not be missing; Patrolman Stettin had been mugged near where Jo-Jo Olsen worked; and Jo-Jo did his fade-out the morning after Stettin had been attacked. It could be something. It could be nothing.

'Did Jo-Jo need money? The cycle must have cost,' I said.

'Jo-Jo stashed his loot. He's a good mechanic. Schmidt pays him good, 'n he don't got to give money home.'

'Did he need a pistol? Maybe he was going into business.'

'Hell, no!' Petey said quickly. 'Anyway, his old man got guns. He could of got a gun.'

'Did he ever have any trouble upstairs? Psycho? Any time on the funny farm?'

'No,' Pete said.

The day was too hot. It was a thousand-to-one that there was no connection between a kid missing a lousy four days, and the mugging of Stettin. But a thousand-to-one is still only odds. It is far from an impossibility. Jo-Jo did not sound like a bad kid, but, then, Pete Vitanza was his friend. Jo-Jo did not sound like a boy with any reason to do a rabbit act. He sounded like a hardworking, ambitious kid. He even sounded a little too good for Chelsea right then and there.

'On the day Stettin was hit, last Thursday,' I said, 'were you and Jo-Jo at the garage all the time?'

'Up to maybe six o'clock.'

I did not know the exact time of Stettin's mugging, but from the rumours it figured to be between 5.30 and 7.30 p.m.

'You were together the whole time?'

Pete Vitanza's Adam's apple worked again. 'We took turns riding the bike. I mean, we was testing it, working it. Maybe we'd be gone ten, fifteen minutes sometimes.'

'Out of sight?'

'Yeh.'

'You think he saw something he shouldn't have?'

His Adam's apple did a dance. 'I don' know, Mr Fortune. Only I know he wouldn't of faded this week-end for nothin' except some bad trouble. When I seen him Friday mornin' he was scared, you know? I mean, he said he couldn't work none, he had some business.' And the scrawny kid looked at me out of those dark eyes. 'Maybe he needs some help, Mr Fortune. I mean, you got to help him, find him. I can pay.'

I like to think I had decided to help Petey before he said that. Like most men who despise money, I always need some. But I know I wasn't considering the money angle at that point. How much could a slum kid have anyway? No, I had already decided to help, I know I had. I had nothing better to do, and I was pretty sure then that it was all nothing. Jo-Jo was on a binge. Maybe away in the hay with some juvenile Jezebel. Boys don't tell each other everything. But it was important to Pete; he was sweating in his chair. As my cases go it was no worse than usual. A boy wanted to help his friend. It was better than most of my cases, and I could always use money.

'I'll check it out,' I said. 'How much can you pay?'

'Would fifty bucks be okay? I mean, for a start?'

I get five dollars for a summons and two dollars an hour for guard work. Industrial snooping pays better, plus expenses. For just about anything else I get what the traffic will bear up to maybe twenty-five dollars a day. Chelsea is not a haven of the rich. The kid surprised me by having fifty dollars. I didn't think that there would be more.

'Tell me more about Jo-Jo. Other friends?'

'We ain't got a lot of friends. Jo-Jo he's kind of a loner, you know? We works mostly on motors. I asked around some.'

'I'll start from scratch,' I said. 'Girls?'

'Nothin' special. Maybe some I don' know about.'

'You mentioned a Driscoll?'

'Nancy Driscoll. She's older like. Only she ain't a real girl friend. I mean, she chased him, you know?'

'Where do I find her?'

'I don' know. I ain't seen her in a while. I figure Jo-Jo been keepin' her under wraps from me, you know?'

'Where did he play cards, shoot dice, drink, have his fun?'

'Jo-Jo don't gamble. He likes movies. He drinks a lot o' places. Maybe by Fugazy. He goes to dances by Polish Hall. He goes to the Y. He goes by the Y alone; I don' swim.'

'Give me a list; anyone and anywhere. His home address. You got a picture?'

'I figured you'd want that,' Pete said.

He handed me a small snapshot. It was poor, but it showed Pete with a motorbike and a tall, blond, good-looking boy of the same age. It would have to do. After Pete gave me the list of names and places, I sent him home.

I called Marty. I had fifty dollars and first things first, right? She was friendly but busy.

17

'New girls at the club, baby, I have to rehearse,' Marty said, 'I'll see you at five, okay? Don't spend the fifty.'

It left me with a free afternoon. There was nothing to do but go to work. I was not anxious. A boy missing for four days was hardly a hot case. But I was on my way out when the phone rang.

'Fortune,' I said. I waited. 'This is Dan Fortune.'

Silence.

But not quite silence. There was something like heavy breathing. I waited. Nothing but the breathing. I hung up. I suppose I should have sensed something then and there. I did stare at that telephone. But that kind of call happens to someone every day in New York. We've got a lot of cranks.

I went out and walked to the precinct station. That's always the first stop. They had no record on Jo-Jo Olsen, but Lieutenant Marx seemed interested. I wondered some about a kid who had reached nineteen in Chelsea without even a juvenile record of any kind. Not even a prank arrest. It made this Jo-Jo sound even more special. I also wondered why Lieutenant Marx seemed interested. I asked him if Jo-Jo Olsen mean something to him, record or no record. Marx said no. He offered no other comment. The police do not give out free information.

I saw the big man when I came out of the precinct into the hot sun.

He was across the street. He was very interested in the window of a bookstore. Which is one of the things that caught my eye. He did not look like a man who read books, and I was pretty sure the level of his eyes and the angle at which he stood showed that he was not looking at the books at all. He was watching the station-house in the window.

The second thing that caught my eye was his shoes. He had the smallest feet I ever saw on such a big man, and the shoes were those old-fashioned, pointed, two-tone brown and beige the sports wore in the twenties.

I started across the street. He walked away fast. I watched him go and thought about the silent telephone call.

CHAPTER 3

Tommy Pucci was on the bar at Fugazy's. I drank two beers before I started the questions. That is protocol. In Chelsea protocol is as rigid as it is at the Court of St. James, maybe more rigid. With my third beer I asked the question. Tommy wiped the bar.

'I ain't seen Olsen,' Tommy said.

'For the record or for real?' I said. 'Jo-Jo is clean. A friend just wants to find him.'

Pucci thought. It must have seemed safe. 'I ain't seen him in a couple days. I told Vitanza.'

'Tell me something you didn't tell Pete. Any friends, girls, Pete doesn't know about.'

Tommy thought. 'Maybe the Rukowski pig.'

'A girl?'

'Jenny Rukowski. I seen Jo-Jo go out with her sometimes. I never seen Vitanza near her.' Tommy grinned. 'I figure Jo-Jo is maybe ashamed he's seen with Rukowski. I know how he feels.'

'Where do I find her?'

'Wait around. Only she don't come in that much.'

Tommy went to tend to business. Rukowski had to be Polish. Polish meant Roman Catholic. I dropped money and a buck for Tommy and walked a couple of blocks to St. Ignatius (Polish) Roman Catholic Church: Father Martinius Reski.

Father Reski turned out to be an old man who knew Jenny Rukowski all right—a no-good girl who never came to mass. When I told him that I was a cop of sorts, he gladly gave me her address. I think he hoped that Jenny, the tragedy of her poor mother's life, was about to be punished for her wickedness.

The address was near the church. It was the usual shabby tenement. The Rukowskis lived on the third floor. The girl who finally answered my knock was tall and big all round. She looked like she was sleeping off a hippo of a hangover when I knocked.

'Jo-Jo Olsen!' she said when I asked. As if it was a dirty word.

'You do know him?'

Her hair was a dirty blonde and thick. It needed a comb. She was not pretty. She was heavy and ugly and her eyes had a tendency to blink even in the dark hallway. She did not ask me in.

'Put-put-put,' she said. 'Those damned bikes. *Put-put-put*, crap! No kicks. I mean, that creeper never turned on, you know?'

'But he was a boyfriend of yours?'

She giggled. 'You're a sweet one. Hell, man, he was a creep I made it with sometimes before I knew he was a creep. I ain't got boyfriends, if you read me.'

'I read you,' I said. She seemed to have no interest in making it with me even before she knew I was a 'creeper'. I did not know whether to be flattered or hurt. About then I had gotten the message. Jenny Rukowski spent most of her time on Cloud Ninety-seven, and not from whiskey. Whiskey did not reach as high as she lived.

'You know where Jo-Jo went, Jenny?' I asked.

'Went?'

'He seems to be missing, vanished, gone,' I spelled out.

She blinked. 'You're puttin' me on, mister! Jo-Jo? You got to be kiddin'! Jo-Jo a rabbit? Christ, he wouldn't never leave that monkey job. Like he sleeps in the grease pit.' Then she brightened. 'Hey, maybe he got with it, yeh? Maybe he turned on. Turn on, tune in, drop out.'

'How about a girl,' I tried. 'Some girl give him a bad time?'

'Jo-Jo?' She kept saying the name as if not sure just who we were talking about. 'He had his bike, *put-put-put.*'

She seemed to think that sound was very funny. I watched her blink. 'There was a square broad. Old, too. Maybe twenny-five! Only it was the broad was after Jo-Jo, yeh.'

'Does she have a name?'

'Who got a name? Hell, maybe he joined the Vikings.'

'Vikings?' I said. 'A street gang?'

'Man, like you got no education. The Vikings, them old-time guys, you know? I mean, Jo-Jo was hipped on them. Horns on their heads 'n all. Beards 'n horns.'

'The Vikings,' I said. I think I stared. In Chelsea no one cares about the past, not even yesterday. 'He was interested in history?'

But I had lost her again. 'Hey, one arm! Crazy!'

She had spotted my missing arm. Her eyes dilated as she stared at my pinned sleeve.

'Who else knew Jo-Jo good?' I asked.

'One arm!' she said. 'Like crazy.'

'You can count,' I said. 'Now tell me more about Jo-Jo.'

'Beards 'n horns. Crazy.'

She was gone. I left her dreaming of beards and horns and one-armed men. She had her troubles. She was big and ugly and her home was a sinkhole. Maybe she made a lot of her own troubles, but don't we all when you come down to it? I went down and out into the heat and sun.

I walked across town to Water Street and Schmidt's Garage. Schmidt wasn't there. The garage office was locked. Schmidt had not replaced Jo-Jo. I studied my list. Both the YMCA and

Automotive Institute were up on Twenty-Third Street. My feet hurt already. I took a taxi.

The Automotive Institute was closest to the river, and the cab reached it first. I went in and asked about Jo-Jo Olsen. They handed me over to a thin, pale man who wore glasses and a snarl and was called an instructor.

'No, I haven't seen Olsen! He had an important exam on Friday. He didn't come. He had shop on Saturday. He missed it!'

He was annoyed as hell about Jo-Jo. He seemed to think that it all made him look bad. He took it personally. He acted like a man who would enjoy kicking a student out.

'Do you know anyone who might know about Jo-Jo?' I asked. 'Some student, maybe? A special friend?'

'Rhys-Smith,' the instructor said. 'He might know what Olsen was up to. Not that I don't know what Olsen is kicking around.'

I perked up my ears. 'You know?'

'Who doesn't? They're all the same. I try to teach them how to be useful. All they want is some floozie. I know Olsen.'

I sighed. Everyone has a hobby horse in his brain. The instructor spent too many hours trying to teach kids who really only wanted to grow up fast and be big men. The instructor was discouraged by too many years of failure. He was bitter. A teacher who had learned that no one wanted to be taught; they just wanted an easy road to easy money.

'What about this Rhys-Smith?' I said. 'Who is he and where do I find him?'

'He's a part-time instructor we use sometimes. You can find him almost any time at The Tugboat Grill. Which is why we only use him sometimes. He knows more about fuel injection than any man in New York, only most of the time the fuel he knows best is alcohol.'

I left the instructor brooding. His real trouble was that he still cared. He cared about Jo-Jo Olsen and all the others. He wanted to teach them, so he hated them. Somewhere deep in the hidden corners of his heart he was a true teacher, and each time one of his boys failed him his heart could not help whispering that perhaps it was, after all, he who had failed.

For Cecil Rhys-Smith the whisper of his own failure had long ago become a shout that could only be lessened by the rush of booze down his always thirsty throat. I found The Tugboat Grill moored at the edge of the river so close beneath the West Side Highway that the shadows of cars flickered the window all day long.

Cecil Rhys-Smith sat on a bar stool with the air of a man who has learned that a bar stool is man's best friend. His beer glass was not quite empty. If the glass had been empty he would not have been allowed to sit there without refilling it. And if he were not there at the bar, how could some generous stranger buy him a drink? It was clear that Rhys-Smith did not have the price of a refill, only the hope. I braced him with the offer of a free whiskey. The suspicion that had begun the instant I had approached him vanished. On the strength of one whiskey and the perpetual hope of one more, he allowed me to take him to a reasonably private back booth.

'Missing?' Rhys-Smith said when I told him about Jo-Jo. 'I had wondered. He's a generous boy for one so young.'

Rhys-Smith looked at my missing arm. 'The young are not often generous, Mr Fortune. Generosity requires some suffering.'

I was not in the mood to tell the story of my arm. Not any of the stories of my arm. So I watched Rhys-Smith. He fitted his name if not his present location. Cecil Rhys-Smith is not a name heard often in Chelsea.

He was a small man, slender and wiry, with the light skin and ruddy complexion of the British Isles. His moustache was thin and pale, and his hair was thin and had once been pale. The hair was grey now, and it looked like he cut it himself. His clothes had once been good tweed. He looked like a man who had once been someone. Not someone important, just someone. He had been a man who had something to do and a place in the world. Now he was no one, and what had happened was as obvious as the shaking of his hands when he tried to sip, not gulp, his free whiskey. Somewhere in his life his way out had become a monster on his back, and he had ended in a cheap bar a long way from home.

'Talk to me,' I said, 'and there'll be more.'

He was not all the way down yet. 'I would talk about my friend Jo-Jo without it, Mr Fortune. I will also take every dram you care to offer.'

'Sorry,' I said.

He shrugged. 'It's a simple life. Only one problem to think about every day, and a good chance that the problem will not last long. But tell me about Jo-Jo?'

'He seems to have vanished. His family say he's just on a trip. Peter Vitanza thinks different.'

'His family, yes,' Rhys-Smith said. 'I never met them. There is some trouble there, Mr Fortune. Jo-Jo was disturbed about his family. I would say that he hated them, and yet, well, he loved them, you see? He is a close-mouthed boy.'

'Where could he have gone?'

'I don't know, but never far from cars or some kind of motor racing. I suppose the Vitanza boy told you of Jo-Jo's dreams? Plans, I should call them. He'll do what he says. All he needs is training and experience. He has the drive.'

'They both do,' I said, and told him about Petey coming to me, and about the fifty bucks.

'A good boy, Petey, but not strong the way Jo-Jo is. Peter has the dreams, not the drive. He's too human, he wants too many other things. Jo-Jo is a rock. Pride if you like.'

'Where do you fit in?'

'I once drove for Ferrari.'

He looked at his empty glass. I waved for another round for both of us. I never let a man drink alone. For a drunk that is demeaning. I'm lucky; I don't depend on a drink. Not yet. My hiding places have not become prisons. That doesn't say that they won't someday, and I try to remember that. A man in prison needs a human word.

'A relief man,' Rhys-Smith said. 'Useful to test the cars. There was the bottle. Once I had ideas. When I did not get what I needed the bottle was the consolation. Now I console the bottle. But I was a driver. I know racing. I know fuel injection. Jo-Jo liked to talk to me. He is a generous boy.'

'Can you give me any leads where he might go?'

'I don't really know much about him beyond his plans.'

'What about women?'

'No, none that I ever saw. He was a remarkably controlled boy. Pete and women, definitely.' Rhys-Smith smiled. 'Pete is like me. Not that Jo-Jo did not have use for a female. But he did not get involved.'

'And Vikings?'

Rhys-Smith laughed. 'Ah, yes, the Vikings. He knew all the sagas. How brave they were, he would say. They could outsail anyone. They had pride, he said, style. Yes, style. He could reel off their names: Harald the Stern, Sweyn Fork-Beard, Halfdan the Black, Harald Fair-haired, Eric the Red, Sweyn Blue-Tooth, Gorm the Old. All they needed was their ship, so Jo-Jo said.'

'That's all? A hobby?'

'He did not like it that his father let people call him *Swede* when they are Norwegians. It seemed important.'

'Maybe he took a trip in a time machine,' I said.

Rhys-Smith smiled politely. He was in that cosy world where it is always warm for a drunk with enough booze. He was feeling fine, and closing time would never come. I slipped a dollar into his jacket pocket when I left. It made me feel big.

Outside the bar I flagged another cab and rode back up to Twenty-Third Street. The McBurney is a big YMCA, but the pool man thought he remembered an Olsen who was a regular. He checked his sign-in sheets for me. Jo-Jo had not missed a week-end at the pool in over a year—until now. Jo-Jo had not signed into the pool at the past week-end.

In the street again I felt half foolish. A nineteen-year-old cuts some classes and a test, leaves a buddy high and dry, skips a big race, and doesn't swim for a week-end. For all I knew, Jo-Jo was on the beach at Atlantic City. There are a thousand things that can make a nineteen-year-old suddenly change his mind, and what is four days?

Marty was waiting for me, and I don't like to keep Marty waiting.

And yet I felt only about half-foolish—Jo-Jo Olsen did seem to be a little missing.

CHAPTER 4

I decided to work on Jo-Jo Olsen a few more days, go through at least the standard routine. Pete Vitanza's fifty was worth that much, and, somehow, Jo-Jo did not sound like he should have done a rabbit. Maybe he had been pushed.

I checked the hospitals, the jails, and the morgue, with no results. They had no Olsen, and only two John Does fitted Jo-Jo's description at all. One was a blond kid off a ship, who turned out to speak no English, and the other was an over-age 'youth' in Bellevue who had been rolled by a sailor and who said that Jo-Jo sounded *darling*. It was slow, hot, tedious work. Do you have any idea how many hospitals there are in New York City with emergency wards?

I tried the taxi companies and the airports. I turned up one lead. A taxi driver had had a passenger early last Friday who he thought had looked something like the picture of Jo-Jo. The driver thought maybe he had taken the fare from Chelsea to the East Side Air Terminal. Some lead.

Bad as the lead was, it ended at the terminal anyway. Even if I could have had a look at passenger lists, I didn't think it would have helped. If Jo-Jo was doing a fade-out, he was sure to be using a phony name.

I put out feelers for information to some of my more reliable connections in the bars, restaurants, bowling alleys, coffee shops, and candy stores in Chelsea, the Village, and Little Italy. I hinted at something being in it for words on Jo-Jo. (For fifty dollars I could not put out much; but, all else aside, most cases in this world are solved by informers, and informers sing only for cash. Eighty per cent of the time police work consists of waiting for a stool pigeon to call.) So I let it be known that I wanted to hear about Jo-Jo Olsen and sat back to wait for someone to come to me and let me earn my fifty.

Two days passed. I had no results from my own hard work. And my feelers turned up nothing at all. No one even whispered to me. I had not really expected the pigeons would sing to me. Not only do I carry the taint of *cop*, despite the old 'pirate' nickname and the ancient history of being like most people in Chelsea, but I don't really belong in Chelsea anymore. I'm not regular. I don't act quite right. I've been away too long and too far.

Over the last twenty years I've lived in a lot of places. In most of the big cities of the world. I'm a city man, that much I know about myself. Big cities: London and New York, Paris and Amsterdam, San Francisco and Tokyo. Sometimes I think that that is about all I do know about myself. At that, it's probably more than most men know about themselves.

In Chelsea most men stay home if they are regular. They set their role in life early, and they don't change it. If a man is a longshoreman, he doesn't sell shoes. If a man is a hustler, he won't pick pockets. A safe-cracker does not strong-arm in alleys. Chelsea likes to know who and what a man is, just the same as the big world wants to know. A man should decide early and for keeps what he will be from the choices he is given. That is what people want in Chelsea, and in the big world. The only difference is that in Cheslea the choices tend to be different.

I've had too many jobs in too many places. I've been a seaman and a waiter, tourist guide and farmhand, private cop and actor, newspaperman and over-age student. Almost any work a man can do with one arm, no special training except in juvenile delinquency, and a useless education. I remember a professor I had out in San Francisco who complained that all I had learned in my haphazard studying didn't add up to a hill of beans. I'm not an engineer or a CPA. I'm not a scientist or a scholar. And I'm overqualified, as they say, to make a good waiter or deckhand. All I had done, that professor pointed out, was learn a lot without increasing my market value.

In Chelsea this adds up to not being regular. When a dockhand knows more than the hiring boss, people are uneasy. I keep my mouth shut as much as possible, and most people in Chelsea don't know my whole guilty secret; but I can't hide it all, and they sense that I don't quite belong anymore. They know that I read books. Reading is one of the dangers of the sea. A sailor has too much time. It is also a danger of living too much alone in strange cities. A man can learn too much by reading. Too much that he can't change and can't forget. They also know that I left Chelsea soon after I lost my arm. They don't know that I've been straight since that day; and they remember the juvenile bandit, but they are not sure about me. They don't know that I came back to Chelsea only because I wanted to stay in one place for a time now and that one of the things I have learned is that it does not matter where a man lives because he lives inside himself anyway and that a man's home is easiest to hide in. But they are uneasy about me sometimes.

I was born in Chelsea, so I'm not an outsider. But, somehow, I'm not quite regular. So I'm in a kind of limbo where people know me, will talk to me, will even help me at times. They will often tell me what I ask, but they will be wary when it comes to talking about someone who might not want me to know what I ask about him. They are not sure about me. And in Chelsea people like to be sure about a man. In fact that was what almost cost Jo-Jo Olsen his life, but I did not know that then.

What I knew was that two more days of work had left me as ignorant about Jo-Jo Olsen as the day I had started and that no one was talking to me about Jo-Jo. I also knew that it was hot, that it was looking more like Jo-Jo Olsen had just taken a trip he had not told Pete Vitanza about, that I could make better use of my time by spending it with Marty, and that I could think of no more good reason to work hard than I could ever think of.

'How about hunger, thirst and me,' Marty said.

Marty is one of the reasons I decided to stay in one place for a while. We've known each other three years now, and her name is on my life insurance. That does not tempt her, which says a lot about her character these days when you read about kids who kill their parents for the insurance money to go to college.

'That's not enough,' I said.

And it's not. A man does not need much money to eat, sleep dry, and get enough to drink to quiet the voices in his head or the pain in an arm that isn't even there. How can something hurt that isn't there? A stupid question. I've read my Freud. What's missing hurts more than anything else, especially when you are alone at night. Sometimes I find myself lying awake and wondering if the arm is still alive somewhere and missing me. I wonder where the arm is now, and if it is lonely. Those are thoughts that can keep a man awake for a long time.

No, I make enough money for my needs. Real work is for something else. Real work has to be for more than a full belly or a paid-up woman. Real work has its own reasons for being done;

reasons that are part of the work itself. That, too, was a fact that Jo-Jo Olsen was going to have to think about before we were finished with each other.

'Are you writing a column,' Marty said, 'or telling about Jo-Jo Olsen?'

Marty likes to read over my shoulder when I write about my work instead of working at it. She has the right.

'Is this about Jo-Jo or about you, Daniel?' Marty said.

'Everything is about me,' I said.

Everything we say or do is really about ourselves. I'm telling my story of Jo-Jo Olsen. The real story. The way it happened to Jo-Jo, and to me. It's not the facts, the simple events, that tell a story. It's the background, the people and what they have inside, the scenery a man lives with, the shadows all around him he never knew were there. The truth does not come in a nutshell.

Give the facts, Marty would say, but what are the facts that made the story of Jo-Jo Olsen? A fact is everything that makes someone act in such a way as to change events. It does not have to be true or logical or something you can point to and put your finger on. There were already two important facts in Jo-Jo's story that had no relation to Jo-Jo at all, but without them there would have been no story, or at least a different story.

One fact was that Pete Vitanza had broken the rules of his brief life. By the rules of Chelsea, Vitanza should have minded his own business. He should have been silent until he knew more. But he came to me. And that was the second fact—that Pete came to me. If he had gone to someone else who knows how it would have ended? Maybe better and maybe worse. But he came to me because I had known his father, Tony, before Tony Vitanza died building a bridge so that people could get to the beach faster. And because I had known Tony, I suppose I felt I owed Pete a little.

Not much, but enough to work a little harder than I might have otherwise.

The story of a man is what that man is. It is the people he knows and loves and hates. The air he breathes. The strangers he never knew existed. The whole complex of shadows waiting for a spark to set them off. The story is that complex, not the spark that blows it up. And Jo-Jo's story is my story. Without me it would have been a different story.

It would also have been a different story if one of the cast of characters had been smarter and less nervous.

I had worked for three days and was about to call it fifty dollars' worth when the spark reached me, and the first blood in the story was mine.

CHAPTER 5

The man who came out of the alley to maul me was big but slow.

'Lay off Jo-Jo!'

I'm not big, and I'm not slow. About five-foot-ten, 160 pounds, and a face that is not the dream of even an ugly schoolgirl. (Especially an ugly schoolgirl. The ugly look for beauty. The beautiful don't have to look for it in others.) But I can catch a fly in mid-air, and when I was a kid I ran the hundred in eleven seconds flat. I've run it faster since when there was no one to clock me except a shadow with hot breath behind me. When you have the average number and size of muscles, no fighting skills except cunning, and you've picked up a handicap like one arm along the way, you have to develop good legs and quick wits. It's called compensation or adaptation or just learning to use what you have.

'Lay off Jo-Jo!'

As I said, he was big but slow. He was also anxious. His first punch got my left shoulder. It was a good punch and would have paralysed my left arm if I had had a left arm. He only got the left shoulder because he had lunged off balance the way a man will who has been waiting too long to throw the punch. He was no trained fighter, but he had muscles. His fist felt like a small bowling ball. I bounced off a wall like a duck pin. His second punch was slow in coming. I had time to roll with it. That was lucky, because it was aimed at my chin and was a lot more accurate.

His trouble was that he had his message on his mind. Any good fighter, ring or street, will claim that to fight well you must have your mind on your work. The fighter who sees the crowd or keeps one eye out for the cops is a loser. His mind was too busy.

'Lay off!'

I rolled with the second punch, that came too slow. I threw one short jab at his face just to slow him down, kicked his shin as hard as I could, and rolled two garbage cans into his path. He ducked my punch, howled when I got his shin solid, and sprawled over the garbage cans when he tried to get at me again. By the time he picked himself up I was nothing but heels going away fast. I think I was leaning on the bar in Packy's Pub and halfway through my first whiskey before the big man knew for sure that I was gone. And my brain was at work. Because I had a clear picture in my mind—a picture of the big man's feet and shoes.

I suppose I saw the shoes when the big man went down over the garbage cans. They were the ancient, pointed, two-toned brown and beige shoes the fashion-plate hoods used to wear in the twenties and thirties. Legs Diamond and oh you kid. And the feet on the big man were like doll's feet. They were, of course, the shoes and feet of the man I had seen outside the precinct station on Monday. Which meant that the big man had been watching me three days. That figured, because he had known that I frequented Packy's Pub, or he could not have been in the alley where he had been. He had probably made the silent call, too. All I had out of it was a cut lip that oozed blood, but I wanted to know who the man was.

'A big guy,' I said to Joe and Packy Wilson. 'Blond or going grey. It was dark. A square face, big and flabby, with jowls and small eyes. A good enough suit, and some kind of accent. He wears small shoes for such a big man. The pair he had on were pointed, two-toned brown and beige. He needed spats.'

Joe thought hard. Joe has worked in most of the saloons in Chelsea, and he drinks in most of the others.

'I don't place him,' Joe said. 'He don't drink around here.'

'If he's who I think,' Packy Wilson said, 'he drinks in the good places. The clubs over in the Village and Little Italy. Maybe the Fifth Avenue places and even uptown.'

'Has he got a name,' I said, 'or do I have to guess?'

'Olsen,' Packy said. 'Lars Olsen. They call him Swede.'

I did not need a sworn statement to know that the big man was Jo-Jo Olsen's father. It made me think. There is a big difference between telling a friend like Pete Vitanza to mind his own business and trying to stop me asking questions about Jo-Jo by using his fists on my skull. It is a matter of degree, of importance. Swede Olsen really didn't want anyone nosing around after Jo-Jo. Why?

'Lend me your gun,' I said to Joe.

I don't carry a gun. It's too dangerous. When you carry a gun you get to depend on it too much. Sooner or later you will use it. A man with a gun is a marked man. I'm a fair shot, but I don't want to prove it and find out the hard way that the other man is better. A gun ruins the brains. But sometimes it can be a needed convincer. Olsen had already jumped me once.

'Be careful,' Joe said.

I put the .38 Police Special in my belt. The night street was as hot as it had been at noon. Pete Vitanza's list gave Olsen's address as on Nineteenth Street, not far from Packy's. I assumed that Swede would have gone home to clean off the garbage. Not that I felt the need for revenge. As far as I was concerned, Swede Olsen could go his way unchastised by me. I would be glad to never run into the Swede, or Norwegian, again. The gun was just for show. If it came to a fight, the odds were still all on his side.

But if I was going on I had to talk to Swede sooner or later, and I could not let him think he had scared me, even if he had. That's bad business and bad living.

It's not so important to win a fight, but it is important to not let the other man win. I wanted Swede to get the idea that I'd get up each time he knocked me down. The fight wouldn't end. That's the best way to make a man stop knocking you down— make him know that it won't get him what he wants. And I wanted him to know that I knew who had jumped me. I'm supposed to be a detective, and it might worry him to think that I knew my work.

The building was not too bad, and not too good. The usual six-storey old-law tenement with the fire escape in front. There were worse on the block, and there were better. It had been worked on some, but it had not exactly been renovated. In the white-tiled vestibule I studied the doorbells and mailboxes. I got a kind of surprise. The Olsens lived on the top floor, which is the cheap floor in a six-storey walkup. But from the look of the mailboxes they had the whole floor. That made their place the best apartment in the building, or at least the biggest. In this building, unrenovated, there were four to six apartments on each floor. The Olsens had a whole floor. Olsen had his name on all four mailboxes of the top floor. It meant that there was money around somewhere. It made them look like pretty fair-sized fish in a small and shabby pond.

From what Petey Vitanza had told me I'd already figured that the Olsens, except Jo-Jo, were not exactly a hard-working family. If they were parasites on some gaudier fish, it looked like that other bigger fish was making pretty big waves. While I was pressing another bell on the first floor I remembered Swede's shoes and his decent enough suit and the information from Packy Wilson that Olsen drank in the better places.

The door buzzed to let me in, and I whipped through the downstairs hall fast. I waited out of sight on the first landing until the irate woman I'd buzzed on the first floor finished muttering a few obscene remarks on the ancestry and occupations of what she supposed had been the kids of the neighbourhood. When her door finally closed I started up the stairs. Not as quietly as a cat, but quiet.

Whatever else he was, Swede Olsen was not worried enough or cautious enough to wonder how come his upstairs bell rang without the downstairs bell. You can usually count on that in New York, because I never saw a building where the downstairs bells always worked or where the downstairs door wasn't either broken half the time or left open to air out the hallways.

Swede opened the door himself and right away. He was my man. The suit had been changed, but the shoes were there on the small feet. The white of the shoes was stained with a mixture of coffee grounds and soggy orange peels. He was a big man, the face was square, and the blond hair was four-fifths grey. His hands were big and fleshy. There was discoloration on the knuckles of his right hand that would be a bruise tomorrow. His complexion was pale from too much time in places with dim light and no air. He was surprised. Even shocked. Me he hadn't expected.

'Dan Fortune, remember?' I said. 'Coffee looks good on the shoes.'

His jowled face went a bright shade of magenta. He clenched his bruised fist. I opened my suit jacket and displayed the police special. He took a step in my direction. I dangled the gun. I didn't point it, you understand, I waved it lightly around under his nose, which was six inches above mine. He was a slow thinker. The danger was that he would start swinging before he thought it out. A smarter type would maybe have guessed that the last thing I would do was use the gun. With Swede the risk was that he would figure he could hit me before I used the gun. But the danger passed. His small eyes blinked at the gun and he stepped back. My diaphragm relaxed. He let me walk into the apartment.

'What the hell do you want, Fortune?'

'Some talk,' I said. 'It was too dark where we met last. Besides, we were both too busy in the alley.'

The apartment was big and ugly, just like Swede Olsen himself. Walls had been knocked down to make one large apartment out of the four small ones, but all they had accomplished was to make a big box out of small boxes. The place was not lack-of-money ugly; it was plain rotten-taste ugly. The whole place shouted of money made too late to know how to spend it. The living-room had cost a lot to furnish, but it still looked like the cheap room it was. The decoration was the kind they used to ship out to Africa to cheat the natives out of their ivory and gold. The couch and two chairs were purple-red velvet with gargoyle wooden legs. All covered with plastic to protect the beauty.

'You crazy?' Swede said. 'I never saw you before.'

He was a terrible liar. He had known me on sight.

'Then you don't mind telling me about Jo-Jo,' I said.

It confused him. His fists began to clench again. I guess that every problem that ever faced Swede Olsen had been met with his only argument—clenched fists. This time even he seemed to sense that he was not reacting very consistently.

'What about Jo-Jo,' he said cautiously.

'Where is he, Swede?'

It was too much for him. 'I told you to lay off!'

'I thought you never saw me before?'

He blinked like a moth in a sudden light. His confusion was complete. I had a good chance of getting something out of him. The woman who spoke behind me must have thought the same.

'Get out of here, mister.'

She looked like one of those Okie women you see in the pictures of the Dust Bowl in the Depression standing beside a grey and battered flivver piled with the junk that was all she owned. Her face looked like a ploughed field that had baked as hard and dry as stone in the sun. Her hair had started out blonde, and her eyes were washed-out blue. The eyes were now glacier blue, and the hair was grey and hung like limp string. Her hands were cracked like a dried-out mud puddle. But her clothes had cost a fair bundle, and the hands were clean. Her black sheath dress even had some style and taste, except that on her it looked like the shroud of a scarecrow. On her the triple strand of real pearls looked like rope. The years had left her nothing to hang clothes on but a bag of old bones and a leather skin.

'I'll handle it, Magda,' Swede said.

His voice would not have convinced even me. The woman ignored him. I knew who was the real muscle in this house. Magda Olsen. The wife. She looked like Swede's mother, but she was his wife, the mother of Jo-Jo. Magda had not had a rosy youth. She looked at me as if I were a cockroach she knew too well.

'Forget my boy, you hear?' Magda Olsen said.

'What's his trouble, Magda? Maybe he needs help.'

'Get lost.'

'You don't want him found?'

'Who says he's lost,' the woman said.

'I say he's lost,' I said. 'What I can't say is if it's voluntary or with some persuasion.'

'Beat it,' Magda Olsen said. She had a one-track mind, and she was brighter and quicker than her man. She knew that I knew nothing. She was not about to tell me anything. I decided to shoot in the dark. One thing was sure: if they knew anything, they knew more than I did. The dark was all I had to shoot in. But I knew now that something was not right with Jo-Jo. I thought about the most probable reason for Jo-Jo to run—that he had seen who mugged Stettin. In which case, someone else would be after him.

'The other guy looking for Jo-Jo will play a lot rougher,' I said. 'If I found him, I could help.'

It was at this exact moment that I knew I had a real case on my hands. I was not just wasting time on a boy's bad hunch, and Jo-Jo Olsen was not sunning himself on a cosy beach. My wild shot hit home.

Swede looked like he'd been kicked in a tender place. Magda Olsen froze into stone. Swede sweated through the fresh suit jacket. Swede was worried wet. Magda was worried, too, but she was also determined. She was determined to follow the course of action they were on, whatever that was. And I had a strange feeling about Magda and Swede Olsen. Call it a sensation. Call it an opinion. They were worried, yes. But they were not worried about Jo-Jo. They were worried about themselves.

'Tell me about the other guy,' I said.

'Beat it,' Magda Olsen said.

'Did Jo-Jo see that cop mugged?'

'Get lost, mister!' Magda said.

If I had had Swede alone, I think I could have made some progress. As it was, I was ready to go on with the dance. I did not have the chance. Two men entered from some other room, and the music stopped. They were boys, not men, but they were big boys. They looked enough like Swede to tell me that I was looking at two of Jo-Jo's brothers. There was a girl behind them. The girl was pretty. The boys were not.

'Take off,' one of the blond boys said.

'My mother said get lost,' the second giant said.

I had the pistol in my belt. I did not even show it this time. The two boys looked about as dumb as Swede, and they did not have his forty-odd years of learning that caution pays. They had not had all the long, hard years to develop doubts. They would not hesitate. I turned without a word and went.

I left them all there in that gaudy sewer of a living room, standing in a line like a firing squad. The boys and Swede were all broad grins. My back going away without a fight made them feel big and strong. The women were not grinning. The ruined face of the mother was as stony as ever above that expensive black dress. As I reached the door I glanced back and saw the old woman already talking hard to Swede.

Then I saw the girl. She had to be Jo-Jo's sister. I saw her eyes watching me. I had the sudden impression that she was the only one of them who was not completely happy to see my back.

CHAPTER 6

In the hot summer nights of New York 4 a.m. is the bad time. The bars and clubs close at 4 a.m., and then there is no more escape from the heat and no more escape from the troubles that follow a solitary man. Four o'clock in the morning is that final moment of truth—the time when there is nowhere else to go but home. If a man has a home.

For me, though, 4 a.m. is one of the good times. When the bars and clubs close Marty has time for me. I often find myself waiting with the last sad drunks for four o'clock. They wait with fear, and I wait with anticipation. It gives me an edge. It makes me feel smug. We are all human. I have somewhere to go, and the wait until 4 a.m. is long. I had a lot of time to consider what I had learned. I did not even feel much like drinking, but the Riviera Tavern was air-conditioned. So I drank slow beers while I waited and considered.

I knew no more than when Petey had come to my office about where Jo-Jo was or why. But it did look like Jo-Jo was really missing and not just on vacation. The Olsens were not surprised at the thought that I was not the only one looking for Jo-Jo. The only apparent reason for Jo-Jo to be wanted was that he knew something about Stettin and that he was afraid for his life. Would a man who had only mugged a cop and left him alive then risk the chair by killing a witness? Would the mugger turn assault into murder? You're damned right he would. It's one thing to commit a crime without murder when you expect to get away with it and another thing to face a sure prison term if you leave a witness alive.

Yet I did not like the answer that Jo-Jo had witnessed the mugging of Stettin.

It was not enough. In Chelsea the best kid in the world has it from the cradle that a man does not fink to the police, does not get involved, does not see what he should not see. (Not just in Chelsea these days, either. Nobody gets involved, nobody sees, everybody turns and walks away.) How different could Jo-Jo be? If he were so different that he rejected the entire code of Chelsea, then the simple act was to go to the police. He had not gone to the police, and he had vanished, and there had to be more than the witnessing of a mugging. But what? What was so very special and dangerous about Stettin's mugging? If that was the problem at all.

Four o'clock came at last, and we were all sent out into the night. My fellow last-ditch drinkers shuffled off slowly to reluctant destinations or to no destination at all. To some alley or doorway where they could hide until the bars opened again.

I walked briskly, I felt smug, I was sober, and Marty should be home by now. And I continued to think about the Olsens. They were worried. But not about Jo-Jo. I was certain of that. They were worried about themselves. As if they were in some kind of collective trouble. I did not think it was police trouble. They were angry-worried, not scared-worried. They were like people on eggshells. They acted as if they did not want to breathe if breathing would expose them. Why?

I was coming up with a lot of questions and few answers. What was there about their missing son that worried the Olsens so much? Concern, yes, that I would expect. But the Olsens did not seem concerned about Jo-Jo; they seemed concerned about themselves. They seemed worried about anyone looking for Jo-Jo—for what it would do to them, not to Jo-Jo. And then I could have it all wrong. Maybe they were just protecting Jo-Jo.

I felt uneasy. The night was hot, and as I walked I did not feel good. Questions without answers make me uneasy. Key questions that I can't get a grip on, that keep slipping away, make me as uneasy as hell. It is like looking into a dark abyss and wondering what monsters might be lurking down there. Monsters that might be waiting for me. Nobody likes the unknown.   —

'You look terrible,' Marty said at the door. 'Come on in.'

Martine Adair. That is her name on the off-Broadway theatre programmes and on the semi-nude come-on posters outside the tourist club on Third Street. It is not her real name. Her real name doesn't matter. She changed her name for a new identity, and I tell stories about how I lost my arm because I don't like the real story. Marty is twenty-seven. Young but no kid. She has not been a kid since she was sixteen. She's a good actress and an adequate girl-show dancer. Her work is more important to her than anything else in the world. The acting, not the girl-show. She studies hard. She has a reason to work. She acts because she must act, for its own sake. And she is good. Someday other people may even know that.

'Irish?' she asked.

'Beer. It's hot enough to boil whiskey.'

'Not in here it isn't. In here it's cool. Respect my air-conditioning; it cost plenty.'

She brought my beer from the kitchen. Her pyjama top came down to the bottom of her white panties. Marty wears only white underwear. She says she gets sick of coloured skivvies in her money work. She never wants to see a spangle or a fringe anywhere in her apartment.

'With the beer I'll be cool inside and out,' I said.

Her apartment is a big, rambling affair. A typical Village apartment: old, inadequate, comfortable, and expensive. The furniture was added one piece at a time because she wanted each piece for itself. Antiques are her major hobby. She refinishes them herself. (That is one of the moments I will remember no matter what happens to me in the end: Marty in a white shirt smeared by wood stain, her face dirty, her hands the colour of old leather, her small body encased in torn dungarees, her hair in her eyes, the eyes bright as she works over an old table she loves.)

She is a small girl, and the hair in her eyes is red just now. It has been other colours in our three years. She has big eyes and a small face that could be the face of a boy. Her mouth is her gimmick—the mouth of a sad little boy on her woman's body, and the combination makes the drunks drool. Her manner is brisk. She strides when she walks. Her walk is almost a run. She does everything fast and eager. She is very alive, and she looks too young for me. She is not too young, but she will probably ruin me.

'Bring me up to date,' she said. 'Who hit you?'

We were on the couch that she bought at a sell-off of old hotel furniture. It is big enough for a giant to stretch out on, if there were any giants any more. I like that couch. I lay at one end, and Marty lay at the other. Our legs touched. I told her about Swede and the Olsens. She frowned.

'Can you drop it? It has a smell, a stink.'

'I took the fifty. I'll go a little longer.'

'This Jo-Jo has trouble, baby,' she said. 'He took his own way out. Maybe he doesn't need you.'

I said that she changed her name because she wanted a new identity and that I tell stories about my lost arm because I don't like the real story. Those things are only partly true. She changed her name for a new identity, yes, but also to forget the old identity.

She wanted to shut out the past because her past, her childhood and her family, was her trouble. I tell stories about the arm not so much because I'm ashamed of the real way I lost it, but because how I lost it is part of my youth. My youth is one of my troubles. So when I see people stare at my missing arm I tell yarns.

I tell them that I lost it on Normandy Beach with the first wave under that terrible fire. I was in the OSS and lost it trying to assassinate Hitler. I was trapped in a sinking submarine and had to cut the arm off to free myself and reach the surface. I tell it many ways, most of them involved with the war, and, strangely, my listeners usually believe me. I suppose we all really want to believe what we are told, and the war is a long time ago now. My lies are as real now as the true stories, even to the men who were there. All my stories are exciting, even heroic. Why not; people like heroes and excitement even second hand in a tavern. Actually, of course, I never made the war, since the arm was gone by then, except on merchant ships, which is how I started on the sea.

None of that is the point. The point is that Marty understands troubles and the way people use to solve troubles. She understands a man's way out; she has her own. She does not go around knocking anyone's way out. She knows that some use whiskey and some use women, that some use junk and some watch TV ten hours a day, that some turn on with pot or acid and some beat their kids, that some chase girls up dark alleys and some chase boys. She knows that most of us use some kind of act, some mask we show the world and usually come to believe is our real face after all. She knows that everyone has a hideout. The hideout can be a saloon or a needle in the vein. It can be a bowling alley twice a week or a bridge club every day or a fraternal club where they wear silk robes and funny hats and give ritual oaths and passwords. It can be the Nazi Party or the Fascist Party, a tree house or just the upstairs back bedroom. She knows that the hideout can be a dream or just a dark place inside a man that comes out alone in bed in the dead of night. She knows her own hideout, and she knows that one of mine is the stories of my arm.

It was the stories that first made her look at me. They intrigued her; she recognized them as a hideout. The first weeks she made me tell her every story I could dream up. Except the real one. She only let me tell her the real yarn a long time later, after I had the key to her apartment. We still lie around in bed and she makes me tell a story. She always acts as if she believed the story. I suppose because she knows that, in a way, I almost believe them myself. Why not? As Marty says, what is true when you come down to it? Especially what is really true that we tell, or know, about ourselves?

'Jo-Jo has no troubles,' I said. 'Not to hear Petey Vitanza tell it, and not that I can find.'

'A good boy who saves his money, has ambition, and works hard,' Marty said. She sipped her martini. 'But he's run, and his father tries to beat you to stop you finding him.'

'To stop me from even looking,' I said. 'There's a difference. He wants me to stop looking.'

'No one knows everything about someone else,' Marty said. 'This Jo-Jo is in trouble the Vitanza boy doesn't know about.'

'Sure,' I said, 'but what?'

'Look at his dream and his family,' Marty said. 'One or the other, and sometimes both. You take me, Dan. Sixteen and a lush for a mother, and the college boys treated me like dirt because I was a town girl and not sorority. I decided to be free and famous. A hundred-to-one it's the family.'

'Patrolman Stettin is in it somewhere,' I said. 'Maybe.'

'And you get mixed up in a cop beating for fifty bucks?'

'Maybe Jo-Jo's already dead,' I said. 'Damn it, Marty, I can't even buy that. All he had to do was go to the cops. They'd have had a cop mugger so fast no one would have noticed Jo-Jo.'

'So what are you going to do? You decided to be a private cop.'

'I decided to eat,' I said. 'A private cop was the only experience I had to sell around here. If I went back to sea, who would take care of you?'

'The way you take care of me you could have picked up coins in the street. But go ahead, worry about who would take care of me. I like you to worry about that.'

'You sound like you want me to make you honest.'

'Maybe I'm getting domestic,' she said. 'Or just tired.'

'That'll do it,' I said, 'and don't scare me.'

'Would it scare you so much?'

'No,' I said, 'and that's the part that really scares me. I might even like it.'

'I wish I could put your arm back,' Marty said.

She was lying there in the dark of the big room, smiling at me from the far end of the couch. Face to face ten feet apart with our legs touching. I touched her leg with my hand. She sipped her martini.

'No one can put back what's missing, but you put me back into the world,' I said.

'Is that what I do?'

She does. Sometimes Marty is the only reason I can think of for getting out of bed in the morning. Sometimes even Marty isn't reason enough. I get out of bed anyway. There is a very big question in that fact somewhere.

'Let's go to bed,' she said.

It takes a one-armed man longer to undress. Marty's bedroom is large, and the bed is king-sized. There is a radio on the bed table and a TV set for watching when she is alone. A neon sign in the street below blinks red and yellow most of the night. Marty likes the blinking sign below, and she likes the noise of a jukebox that filters up. She is afraid of the dark, of hearing no sounds and no voices. She is afraid of going to sleep. In bed she laughs a lot. She plays games. But when the games are over she holds me tight. I know the feeling. I know the need and the fear that fills our world. And now I found myself wondering what Jo-Jo Olsen needed and where he was. I waited in the bed for Marty and wondered if Jo-Jo, too, was lying in some bed somewhere needing voices, afraid to sleep.

'Dan.'

Her voice was low. I looked. I expected to see her face close in the dark with the expression that she wanted me. She was not close. She was at the bedroom window looking down at the dark street. I got out of bed and went to her. She held the heavy drapes open a crack.

'There,' she said.

At this hour the street was all dark. The neon sign had gone off, the jukebox was quiet. It was the edge of morning, and a faint grey tinged the sky to the east. The street itself was the deep black that precedes the dawn. But I saw them.

'Yes,' I said softly.

There were two of them. Shadows hidden in a recessed doorway across the street. I knew them. Not their names and not their faces, but I knew them. If we had been in some other country they could have been secret police or assassins waiting for some leader of men. They could have been the thin and starved rebels in too many countries where tyranny still rules. Here and now, on the Village street, they would be none of those things. They were hoods, gunmen, muscle boys; the soldiers of an underworld that was the shame of the country. And from where they waited they had a clear view of only one building—Marty's building.

'All right,' I said. 'They must be after me. They won't try to come in.'

'Dan, I don't like it.'

'Neither do I,' I said. 'Let's go to bed.'

The ways of fear are strange. We wanted each other.

Marty went to sleep just as the dawn came. I lay awake. The two men down there in the street made all this something else.

I wondered what I had got into for fifty bucks and a kid who wanted to find his friend?

CHAPTER 7

The ringing of the telephone woke me up at ten o'clock. Marty was still asleep, and I wished I was. But I groaned my way to the telephone. The voice on the other end was unfamiliar and official. It identified itself as a Lieutenant Dolan, New York City Police Department, and its message was that Captain Gazzo wanted to see me—now.

I hung up and went back to the bed wondering if this was it. Had they found Jo-Jo? Floating in the river? Under a pile of old garbage in a cellar? I had no doubts what Gazzo wanted to talk about. My feelers on Jo-Jo would not have gone unnoticed at headquarters. And Gazzo is Homicide. I looked at the bed, and my whole body groaned to get back in and vanish under the covers. Instead, I took a deep shudder to try to wake up and touched Marty.

She snarled and burrowed deeper into the pillow. She does not like to wake up any more than she likes to go to sleep. Under the sheet she was small and slender and pale. At that moment it did not seem that there could be anything important enough to leave her for. And yet I would leave. If I could.

I went to the window to check. My two shadows were still there. In a way I felt for them; it must have been a long night. I dressed and went to kiss Marty. She swore at me and flopped over.

'Don't open the door to anyone you don't know,' I said.

I slapped her rump. She opened one angry eye.

'You got that?' I said.

She closed the one eye and nodded.

I slipped out and went down to the first floor. I took the back way out into the yard. I went over a fence and through the building behind Marty's building and out into the next street. To be sure, I did a few fancy turns around the blocks and through a few more doors and back yards. The heat had instantly drained any desire for breakfast. I settled for two cups of coffee at a luncheonette and took the subway downtown to headquarters.

Captain Gazzo is an old cop. I've know him since I was a kid. He knew my mother, and he calls me Dan if it's not official. He never married; he has only his work. Most of the time he is a good cop, the kind who knows that his job is to help the people of the city, not scare them. He knows that a cop is a necessary evil, and he does not complain often when the rights of citizens get in his way, as they must. But he is human, too, and there are times when the restraints make him swear. There are other times when he says he is crazy, because the world he lives in is crazy and you have to be crazy to handle it. He says that he would not know what to do with a sane person, because he never gets to meet any. He includes me with the insane. Maybe he knows.

Despite the morning hour and the heat, Gazzo's office was dim behind drawn shades. Gazzo says that the sun does not fit with his work. I could tell by the size of his grey eyes that he had not slept well again. There are those who say that the captain never sleeps at all, that he has no bed, that he does not even really have a home. These people say that Gazzo files himself in his own office when other people sleep. But I know that Gazzo has insomnia. He does not hide this. He says that insomnia is the wound-stripe of the cop, the price you pay. He says it just proves that he is human after all.

This morning he waved me to a seat at once. It was an order, not an offer. He wasted no time on preliminaries.

'Before you go into the act about your rights, protecting your client, and all that, I'll give it to you. I know you're looking for a Jo-Jo Olsen. You think he's missing. He works around Water Street. My birds sang that much. Now you'll tell me who, what, when, where, why, and how. Okay?'

That is Gazzo's trademark: he never uses one word when ten will do. He's been called Captain Mouth and Preacher Gazzo, and the word is that when Gazzo starts talking you're dead. They say that Gazzo makes men talk who would have held out under a week of rubber hoses.

'Joseph "Jo-Jo" Olsen,' I said. I never hold out unless I have to protect myself. I never know when I might need the cops.

'Olsen works on Water Street at Schmidt's Garage,' I said. 'He seems to be missing since last Friday morning. I'm trying to find out why and where. A kid friend of his hired me. One Pete Vitanza. So far I haven't found a hair of Olsen.'

'Joseph Olsen,' Gazzo said. He was hearing the name. I could see him run it through the thirty years of police work that was all that his brain contained now. The computer of his mind checked the name against the parade of hoods, con men, hustlers, killers, wife-beaters, muggers, and practitioners of every other crime in the book he had come to know in the thirty years. A card clicked out. 'Any part of Swede Olsen?'

'Son,' I said. 'Swede is hiding him.'

I told him about Olsen's inefficient attempt to beat my brains out last night and a certain amount of my interview with the Olsens. I did not tell him about the gun I had used, and I did not mention my impression that the Olsens had trouble of their own. I also left out the two shadows under Marty's window. Gazzo seemed interested in what I told him, but with the captain you can never tell. I've known him for twenty-five years, and I don't know if he likes me or hates me. With Gazzo it does not matter. He does his job, friend or foe.

Gazzo rubbed the grey stubble of his chin. 'And the kid works at Schmidt's Garage?'

'He did.'

'He was there last Thursday, but gone on Friday?'

'That's it.'

'Interesting,' Gazzo said. 'You have nothing yet on why he ran or where?'

'Nothing,' I said. 'Now tell me what you've got, Captain. You didn't drag me down about some unknown kid. What don't I know? I know about Patrolman Stettin. Is there more?'

Gazzo smiled. 'I thought you gave up on the world, Dan.'

'I try, but it hangs around,' I said. 'What's up, Captain?'

Gazzo pressed a button. A policewoman came in. Gazzo seemed surprised to see her. I know that she has been in Gazzo's office for years. He still looks at her face to see if she needs a shave. He stares at her blue skirt as if sure that something is wrong. Change comes slow in the dim world of Homicide.

'Jones file, er, Sergeant,' the captain said.

Gazzo is resigned to knowing and meeting every perversion and horror man can do to man, but he can't get used to a female sergeant. When she returned he took the file without a smile.

'Tani Jones, not her right name,' Gazzo read from the file. 'Real name: Grace Ann Mertz. Born: Green River, Wyoming. Parents still there. Caucasian; twenty-two years old; blonde; five-foot-eight; 132 pounds. Model and chorus girl. Worked at The Blue Cellar. A tourist club on Third Street.'

Gazzo looked up at me. 'Your sparrow works in one of the tourist clubs, right?'

'Monte's Kat Klub.'

'She know a Tani Jones?'

'Not that I know. When Marty puts her clothes back on she forgets the clubs. When we talk shop, it's acting. Real acting.'

'Maybe this time?' Gazzo said. 'There must have been talk.'

'She doesn't socialize with the club girls, Captain. She spends her time, all she can, with the off-Broadway people,' I explained. 'What is it? Dead? Killed? Some time last Thursday or Friday?'

It was a simple guess. Gazzo is Homicide. He was interested in a boy who was on Water Street on Thursday and gone on Friday.

'Thursday afternoon,' Gazzo said. He went on reading his file. 'Lived alone in a four-room luxury apartment in a non-doorman building on Doyle Street. Self-service elevator. Body found Friday morning by maid who comes in twice a week. Death from single gunshot wound in the head, close range. Gun was a .38 calibre, probably a small belt gun according to ballistics. The place had been cleaned out. A lot of jewellery was gone. Worth maybe fifteen thousand dollars appraised value. There was an insurance list of the jewellery. Her boyfriend also confirmed what was gone and that nothing else had been touched.'

The captain watched me the whole time he read. I could not figure why. Unless he thought I knew more than I did. What could I know? All right, I got the picture now: Doyle Street was the next block to Water Street. But, as I said before, we get fifty violent crimes a day on the West Side, and a robbery killing doesn't rate more than a couple of inches in most papers except the *Daily News*. I don't read the *News*. I read the crime news in the better papers, sure, but I've got my own interests, and if I'm not hired for a job, why would I connect a two-bit killing on Doyle

Street with a cop mugging on Water Street? I mean, Doyle is a long street.

'I suppose the building on Doyle backs towards Water Street?' I said. 'Same crosstown block as Schmidt's Garage on Water?'

'With an alley on the side that opens into both streets,' Gazzo said.

I thought about the city. Most cities have slums and middle-class areas all properly separated. The rivers make Manhattan special. Manhattan is an island, and there is little space to move in. The result is that the city moves in circles from good to bad and back to good again. You end up with a city in constant flux; with tenements, businesses, private houses, small factories, and luxury buildings all mixed together. And new buildings on polyglot streets are prime targets for burglars.

'She caught a burglar in the act?' I said.

'That's the way it reads,' Gazzo said. 'Door was locked and on the chain. The maid had to go to the back entrance. The back door was open, the lock cracked. The back door opens into a service stairway that goes down to the alley and a basement garage. The alley opens into Doyle Street at one end and Water Street at the other. No one saw the thief. At least, no one who's talking.'

'Broad daylight?' I said. 'With the woman at home?'

'Her man says Tani was almost always out in the afternoon on her modelling work. Thursday she called in sick and cancelled a date with the photographer. The photographer says she missed a lot of appointments. She wasn't too reliable. The bed had been slept in. She was in her slip, pants, and bra.'

'Has the loot shown up?'

'No,' Gazzo said, and brushed me off. 'Tell me more about this Olsen kid.'

I sensed the change of subject, the brush-off. The captain did not want to talk about the loot. It should have appeared by now. Burglars unload fast. I did not push it. If Gazzo held back, he had his reasons. He would tell me when he wanted to.

'I told you all of it,' I said. 'He's gone, period. A lot of people on Doyle and Water Streets probably went on trips.'

'You think this Jo-Jo saw something?'

Gazzo did not believe that a lot of people from Doyle and Water had gone on trips. Neither did I.

'Jewels don't show, I said. 'Even if the burglar came out on Water Street, all Jo-Jo would see is a man walking around.'

'Maybe he saw the guy in the alley,' Gazzo said.

'Just walking? How would he know?'

'Maybe he saw and recognized the guy. Later he hears about the burglary and killing and puts two and two together. Maybe he knows the guy saw him and knows him.'

It was a good theory. I could believe it. But I fought it for a time.

'So he hangs around from Thursday evening to Friday morning?' I said. 'I mean, if the killer knew him, what held the killer up so long. My client says he talked to Jo-Jo Friday morning. I mean, Jo-Jo was nervous but not hiding yet.'

It stopped Gazzo for the moment. It stood to reason that if Jo-Jo and the killer knew, each other, and the killer knew he had been seen, and Jo-Jo thought there was danger enough to run, then the killer would have tried for Jo-Jo right away Thursday night. The time lag was all wrong—unless? I thought about Swede Olsen.

There aren't many men you would see walking on the street and pay enough attention to, to wonder what they were doing. Especially if you were busy testing a new motorcyle and especially if the man did not want to be seen. But if you saw your father, even a quick glimpse, you'd notice and wonder. For some reason this did not seem to have occurred to Gazzo. And I still did not feel that the Olsens were worried that way, the police-trouble way. Anyway, why would Jo-Jo run if it had been Swede he saw? Not many boys rat on their father. Not every day anyway.

'What about Stettin?' I said. 'Coincidence? Or maybe he saw the burglar?'

Gazzo rubbed the grey stubble of his chin. The captain needed a shave. He usually does unless City Hall or the chief wants to see him. Gazzo took some acid in the face twelve years ago and his skin is tender.

'No one ever accused our men of being slow on the trigger,' the captain said. 'If Stettin had seen anything, there would have been a rumpus. Anyway, he saw nothing.'

'Maybe the burglar thought Stettin saw him.'

Gazzo sighed wearily. 'If the burglar even thought Stettin saw him, would he leave him alive? It was already felony murder.'

'A cop killing? You'd have hounded him past hell.'

'If he thought Stettin had seen him, it was kill or nothing, Dan. Why just tap him and leave him alive to make the ident? It wasn't as if Stettin was chasing him. That might make some sense. If Stettin was after him, he might have tapped him just to get away. But Stettin saw nothing. Not even who hit him.' Gazzo suddenly grinned in the dim office. 'Stettin is embarrassed. It hurt his image of himself to have been slugged and not be able to say who, or even guess why. I think it's the shoes that make him feel worst. He doesn't like it that we found him with no shoes. Good thing he didn't lose his pants.'

Gazzo was right. Stettin did not seem to tie in. So maybe it was still that Jo-Jo had just seen a mugger, not a killer. Or a killer and not a mugger. Take your choice.

'How about some clues?' I asked.

'Clues?' Gazzo looked sour. Clues don't solve cases. 'Sure, one on the Jones girl. A losing stub on a slow horse at Monmouth Park the day before. On the floor near the body. It was all that did not belong to Tani or her lover-daddy.'

'Thanks,' I said.

Monmouth Park is a popular track. I'd hate to be chased down a dark street by half the losers there in a single day. It's like that with clues. Most of the time they don't help, because most murders aren't that logical or planned. Motive, opportunity, and witnesses, that's what convicts.

'What about the timetable?' I asked.

Gazzo checked the file. 'Woman died between five thirty and six thirty in the afternoon. Stettin was hit about six thirty.'

The time was just about as bad as it could be. Jo-Jo and Petey Vitanza had been at Schmidt's until about six o'clock. Time is sometimes a good hammer to hit a killer with, but it's not perfect. I mean, how many times do you really know exactly what time it is or what time you were at any particular spot a day or a week before? Give or take a half an hour is about the best most people can do without looking at their watch. And in this case a half hour made a world of difference. About six o'clock could mean five thirty and the opportunity to burglarize the apartment of Tani Jones.

Gazzo was watching me. 'The Olsen kid play the horses, Dan?'

I stood up, 'Cars and motorcycles are his line. Maybe he is just on a trip.'

I didn't believe that now, and neither did Gazzo.

'Swede Olsen was just trying to insure his boy's privacy,' Gazzo said.

'Maybe he just doesn't want anyone talking to anyone about his family.'

'That much I can believe,' Gazzo said.

I left the captain putting out the call for Jo-Jo Olsen; all points, all cities. Gazzo looked weary behind his desk. His eyes were glazed, turned inwards, as if he was seeing all the nineteen-year-old boys he had had to pick up and lock up in his life. The captain was near retirement, I had heard him talk about it himself. Then he had looked at me and asked what the hell would he do if he retired?

Out in the street I headed for the subway. What I had heard from Gazzo was about as enlightening as everything else I had learned up until now. The more I thought about it, the less I could see Jo-Jo in the robbery or the killing. I did not think Gazzo could either. The police work on patterns, records, facts. Jo-Jo had no record, the pattern stank. In Chelsea every kid is born knowing better than to pull a job on his own block—and then point the finger at himself by running.

I thought about Swede Olsen again, but that didn't play any better. If Swede had killed, he should have run, not Jo-Jo. No, neither of them should have run. The thief and killer had made it clean away; why run at all? Maybe it was Swede, and Jo-Jo was ashamed. Maybe that was the story. Jo-Jo faded to get away from a father who was a thief and killer. It was better than most of the explanations I had had so far. Which shows the quality of my explanations.

On the subway I decided to head for Schmidt's Garage. It was about all I had not done that I could think of now. Not that I was looking for more to do. What I needed was a better theory. I needed a theory of any kind. Right then, let's face it, I had no proof that Jo-Jo was in any kind of trouble, and I could not fit the trouble I had to Jo-Jo. It did not ring true. Jo-Jo did not sound like a burglar. Maybe there was another way to look at the events on

Water and Doyle Streets? As a matter of fact there were a lot of other ways. There was much that I did not like.

I did not like the way Tani Jones had died. The theory of her murder, I mean. You would be surprised how few burglars panic and use guns. Even amateurs or junkies. Jo-Jo was an amateur, but he was not a junkie. At least, I had no word that he was on the fix. Also, assuming that the burglar had for some reason mugged Stettin, he did not sound like an amateur. The mugging had been expert. Of course, there was no real connection so far between the mugging and the robbery, except that they had happened at nearly the same time on adjoining blocks. Still, what I really did not like was the theory of a panicked burglar. Gazzo had made no mention of Tani Jones fighting back, of even having a weapon. About the only time a robbery victim is killed is when he tries to resist, fight.

Professional thieves carry guns, yes, although not as often as you might think. (Blackjacks and iron pipes are more in their line.) And they use them even less often. Felony murder is a hard charge. This burglar had made a perfect entrance and exit. Unseen all the way. Yet the theory was he had been surprised by a woman asleep in the bedroom and had shot. He should not have been surprised, and he should not have shot. Unless Tani had recognized him—and that was something else again.

By the time I climbed out into the ninety-degree cool of Sixth Avenue, I had switched to the other side. Burglars did panic. Junkies could be clever one minute, stupid the next. Accidents happened, and surprised men shot. Unconnected crimes happened within a few feet every day in New York. My brain was still making the circles when I reached Schmidt's Garage.

Old Schmidt was under a car with his pale legs sticking out like those of a chicken. When he heard my errand he crawled out. He was a small, chunky man of about seventy. White-haired and with the ruddy round face of a cherub. There was grease on his face. It was a good face. He reminded me of a little German pastry cook I had known when I was a kid. The bakeries had gone out on strike. The little cook marched in the snow with all the others. He was an old man who should have been home with his pipe, his grandchildren, and his memories. But there was a principle at stake: his fellow men needed him, so he marched. When two company toughs knocked him down he got up and went back to the picket line without a word. Schmidt looked like that kind of man.

'I am worried,' the old man said. 'Jo-Jo is good boy, work hard. He go and he don't tell me? That is funny. I am worried.'

'Kids get ideas. Maybe he just got tired.'

'Not without he tell me, no. And the bike. There it wait.'

The old man pointed to a motorcycle in the corner of the garage. A motorcycle carefully covered by a heavy plastic cover. It shone through the plastic like a jewel. Jo-Jo took good care of his motorcycle.

'I call by his old man,' Schmidt said. 'He say Jo-Jo take a trip. I should mind my sauerkraut. His kind I know, *ja*! I am worried.'

'What do you know about Tani Jones or Patrolman Stettin?'

'The woman who was killed and the policeman? I know what I read, hear. No more. You think Jo-Jo? Never! No!'

'Did he have any trouble you know? Any new friends, maybe? Any girl trouble? A sudden need for money?'

'No. Thursday he work here all day on the bike, Friday he don't come to work. He don't tell me. I don't like that.'

'What about a girl named Driscoll?'

'Driscoll? So? She come here one, maybe two times. She want Jo-Jo. She talk to Petey and Jo-Jo. Jo-Jo go away. He don't want her.'

'Where do I find her?'

Schmidt started to shrug, and then held up a finger. 'Wait, *Ja*! I think . . .'

He skipped away towards the office like a schoolboy. He was a peppery old man. He came back carrying a coloured brochure. I took the brochure. It was a travel piece about Italy. It had pictures of the red Ferrari racing cars.

'She bring for Jo-Jo once,' Schmidt said. He pointed to the line stamped on the back. 'She work there.'

The address was: *Trafalgar Travel Bureau, 52 West 46th Street.*

'*Ja,*' Schmidt said. 'She work there. You think . . .'

I never did learn what Schmidt was about to ask me. The telephone rang. He answered it. I saw the colour spread across his cherub face. When he put down the receiver he was red.

'They beat Petey! Someone! In hospital by St Vincent's!'

St Vincent's was only a few blocks away.

I went out on the run.

CHAPTER 8

They told me that Petey would probably live. They also said that he would even see again. He wasn't blind, it only looked that way. His face wasn't a face now; it was a bandage.

'Both eyes slam shut,' the doctor said. 'Nose busted, cheekbone, too. I never saw more bruises, I tell you.'

There were tubes in Petey, and bottles hanging all over that white room. I saw the morphine Syrette on the side table beside the bed where Petey was half propped up because of the internal injuries. They had broken both arms. The splinted and bandaged arms stuck straight out in front of the boy who had only white cloth where his face had been. But the real damage was the shattered ribs and the internal injuries from the kicks.

'A very complete job,' the doctor said. 'I had a case on the Bowery once, but this is more complete.'

The police were there, of course, since it was pretty clear that Petey had not fallen down some stairs. It was Lieutenant Marx who let me into the room. One old cop agreed with the doctor that it was a hell of a good beating, but the old cop did not think it was professional.

'Amateurs,' the old patrolman said. 'They used their hands and feet. Too much blood and damage without enough pain. It looks like they let him pass out, and kicked him while he was out. That's a hell of a way to get something. Just amateurs.'

'They were after information?' I asked Marx.

'Yeh,' the lieutenant said. 'He couldn't talk, but we asked him and he nodded. We don't know what they wanted to know.'

'Where did it happen?' I said, and then I heard the plural everyone was using. 'They? How many were there?'

'Two,' Marx said. 'We found him over in an alley near the West Side Highway. Some dame called in; no name.' And then Marx eyed me suspiciously. 'What's your interest, Fortune?'

But I was thinking about two men. Two men had beaten Petey almost to death. It had been two men who stood out there in the street last night watching Marty's apartment. I did not need a computer to tell me that the two men, whoever they were, were after Jo-Jo Olsen. I was in something, I did not like it; but I was almost getting mad now as I looked at the bandages and tubes and hanging bottles that were Petey Vitanza.

'He's my client,' I said to Marx.

'This kid?' Marx said.

'He wanted his friend found,' I said. 'Jo-Jo Olsen, remember?'

Marx nodded slowly. 'Yeh, I remember. Funny, but Homicide's got a pickup out on this Jo-Jo Olsen. What did he do?'

'That's what we all want to know,' I said.

'You think the two who worked on Vitanza were after the Olsen kid, too?'

'Maybe,' I said. 'Or maybe they were out to stop anyone from finding Olsen.'

Marx watched me. He was a smart cop. 'You're looking for Olsen.'

'I know,' I said as I looked at the ruin that was Petey Vitanza. There was something like a cold breath that went through that room and along my spine. I only have one good arm; I want to keep it in one piece.

'Keep in the middle of the street,' Marx said. 'Any ideas who the two musclemen were?'

'If I did I'd be howling for the police right now,' I said.

'How come Homicide is on to it?' Marx said. I told you that he was a smart cop.

'They think maybe it's all tied in with the Tani Jones killing,' I said.

Marx was thoughtful. 'They do, huh?'

As I said, the cops give nothing away. That was all Marx said. And my mind was on Petey Vitanza.

'Can I talk to him?' I said.

The doctor shrugged. 'He can't answer.'

'He can nod,' I said.

'Okay. Two minutes; no more. Then everyone out,' the doctor said.

I bent over the bandages. It was like talking to a corpse. Petey could move nothing but his head. But he could hear.

'Did you recognize them at all?' I said.

A negative shake, slow and drugged.

'Did they want to know about Jo-Jo?'

Affirmative, a small nod.

'They did not want you to lay off Jo-Jo? They wanted to find Jo-Jo?'

Affirmative. They were looking for Jo-Jo, not warning off.

'Did Jo-Jo know a Tani Jones?'

Nothing. No movement. Then I saw a faint motion of his shoulders. Petey had shrugged.

'You don't know if Jo-Jo knew Tani Jones?'

Affirmative. He did not know about Tani Jones one way or the other.

'You said Jo-Jo seemed in trouble. Was he scared?'

A faint shrug.

'This Driscoll girl. Was she trouble for Jo-Jo?'

The shrug.

The doctor stepped in. 'That's all.'

Petey became agitated. He wanted to speak. I guessed.

'The Driscoll girl might know something? Might be trouble?'

A quick affirmative.

Then there was a strange movement. The doctor bent over the ruin that was Pete Vitanza. I watched. The doctor straightened.

'Passed out. Everyone out. Out!'

Lieutenant Marx left a man outside the door. Marx and I walked out of the hospital to find that it was still hot, still summer, and still early afternoon. I felt that it should have been night and winter. At the moment I did not care about Jo-Jo Olsen or Tani Jones or Patrolman Stettin or law and order. I cared about Pete Vitanza and the kind of men who could beat a nineteen-year-old boy that badly. I did not want justice, I wanted them. It's like politics with me: I don't care about Antipoverty Programmes with capital letters, but I care about the poor. Then, too, I care about myself. These men were after me. I did not want men like that walking around where I walked.

'Take good care, Fortune,' Marx said as we parted.

The way the lieutenant said that made me stand there in the sun across from Loew's Sheridan and stare after the squad car as it took Marx away. The lieutenant knew something that he was not telling me. Just as Gazzo had known something. I felt that it was about Tani Jones and her killer and why the killer would not fence his loot.

There was something else in all this. A third force of some kind, you might say. I was sure of that now. A third force that had shown so far only as two shadows on a dark street and as two unknown men who had beaten a boy and asked questions. They could be the same two, or a different two. How many there were and who they were, I did not know. I did not like that. As I said, unanswered questions are like lurking monsters. I wanted the answers. At least, as I stood there in the sun I thought I did. It was not long before I was not so sure. I was about to get part of an answer sooner than I had expected.

I went to find Marty. I needed company after Pete, and I wanted to talk about Tani Jones. Marty was out of bed now, and bushy-tailed. She had forgotten the two shadows. They were not in evidence. We went to the sidewalk café of O. Henry's. Marty had a Pernod on ice. I had a beer and a good view of one of the best sights in New York: Marty in a short skirt.

'You are a dirty old man, Dan Fortune,' Marty said.

'Is there another kind? You beautiful young girls won't let us men grow old properly.'

'Am I beautiful, baby?'

'You are to me,' I said, 'and on stage. That's what counts: to your man and in your work, you're beautiful.'

I got a nice smile. She's not really beautiful. She's pretty enough, and she has the body to make any man stare for at least a few minutes. But the real thing is that she is exciting. Pretty is a dime a carload, but exciting comes scarce. She's alive. She never stops moving, not even when she is doing nothing. She keeps me busy—body and mind. But today I had some other problems.

'Did you know Tani Jones, Marty?'

She shook her head. 'No. You know I don't hang around with the girls. She was the girl killed by the burglar, wasn't she? One of the girls was talking about her a few days ago. I never met her. The Blue Cellar is two blocks away. What a shame, Dan. I mean, what a stupid way to die for a young girl.'

'Have any men been hanging around the girls?' I asked.

'Men are always hanging around, I . . .'

Marty stopped. Her wide eyes became wider. She was facing Sixth Avenue, and I had my back to the avenue. I turned to look.

'Hello, Danny.'

He came up and sat down across from me at that postage stamp table. Andy Pappas. The innocent people strolled along only inches away, and Pappas sat there and smiled. Beyond the price of his suit, which had to be at least three figures, Pappas looked like any other man. His homburg was a dark blue, his tropical suit was dark blue with the faintest of conservative pinstripes and a natural-shoulder ivy-league cut. His shirt was good blue-and-white-striped oxford cloth with a relaxed button-down collar as befitted the afternoon and early evening hours of a businessman. His tie was a regimental stripe, and his shoes were a soft and informal black leather. No gun bulged under the slim suit coat.

It's good to see you, Danny. Share a round, right?'

I've known Andy Pappas all my life. We're the same age. We grew up together here at the edge of the river. We learned to like girls at the same time. We graduated from high school in the same class. We danced at the Polish dances and drank wine at the Italian street festivals. We stole together in those early days. Andy knows how I lost my arm. It was his tip that sent Joe and me to the Dutchman ship that night. It was Andy who would have arranged the fencing of the loot if I had not broken my arm.

Maybe all of that is another reason why I tell stories about the arm instead of the truth—the fact that Andy Pappas is a major reason why I am still thought to be in any way regular, the reason I get the benefit of some doubt. In Chelsea no one would, or could, understand that a man could know Andy Pappas and not offer up prayers of thanks every night. That is why Andy survives, grows richer. We were kids together, yes, and that was where it ended.

Joe is poor and hard-working. I am poor and work for a living, if not too hard. Andy is rich, and no one alive knows for sure what his work is.

'The same for my friends, and a little Remy Martin for me,' Andy said to the waiter. The waiter was polite. Andy was polite. He smiled at me again. 'Say hello, Danny.'

Andy Pappas is a boss. A boss, that's all. For the record and the newspapers Pappas is boss of a big stevedoring company on the docks. For the record, and for the sake of all the public people who are supposed to have the power, Pappas runs a good, efficient, profitable, and useful company. Off the record Andy is the boss of something else. There are those who say that he is the boss of everything else. Some even say it out loud. Andy does not worry about that. Everyone knows that what Andy is boss of is illegal, a racket. Only no one really knows just what that racket is, except that a major part of it is keeping the river-front peaceful. Pappas gets the ships unloaded in peace and quiet—for a price. The general guess is that Andy has all, or a piece, of just about every illegal enterprise there is. Of course, the true occupation of Pappas, the true occupation of any boss like Andy, is extortion. That is what a racket is—any activity, legal or illegal, where a major part of the method of operation is fear. Whether it is heroin or just asphalt that the racketeer sells, his main selling method is fear, the fear of harm; extortion.

'Hello, Andy,' I said. I nodded to Marty. I wanted her to leave. Andy smiled.

'Let the lady stay, Danny. I've seen her work. She's too good.' Andy has a nice voice, low and even, and his speech is very good for a boy who only barely got out of high school. Everyone says that he took lessons, but I remember that he always had a good voice. 'Besides, we're old friends, right, Danny?'

'You don't have a friend, Andy,' I said. 'You're the enemy of everybody.'

Pappas nodded. He did not stop smiling. It was an old story with us.

'You don't soften up, do you, Danny?'

'You never change, do you, Andy?' I said. 'This isn't a social visit.'

I nodded towards the lamp-post a few feet away from the table of the tiny sidewalk café. It was one of those old gaslight lamp-posts O. Henry's has put up for atmosphere. Leaning against it now, pretending to watch the little-girl tourists pass, was Jake Roth. Roth was not watching girls; he was watching me. Andy Pappas never carries a gun, everyone says, but Roth goes to bed with a shoulder holster under his pyjama top. Roth is Andy's top persuader. Across the street I saw Max Bagnio. Little Max is the second-best gun, and now was trying to read a newspaper in front of a stationery store by spelling out the words one at a time. Actually, Bagnio was watching me in the store window. And just up the block towards Sheridan Square I saw Andy's long, black car parked in front of a Japanese knick-knack shop. The driver sat behind the wheel with his cap down and his arms folded. I did not need to guess that a gun was hidden under those folded arms.

Pappas had followed my glances at his men. He shrugged.

'You said it, Danny. Everyone is my enemy. A man has to protect himself.'

'That isn't exactly what I said, Andy, but let it pass. What's on your mind?' I asked.

'Drink up first, Danny. You're my friend, if I'm not yours. The lady seems thirsty.'

'I don't drink with you Andy, and neither does the lady,' I said. 'Those days went a long time ago.'

I know I go too far with Pappas. There was that glint in his cold eyes. They are dead, Andy's eyes. The cold eyes of a dead man who long ago stopped asking himself what he really wanted or why he was living. I have seen eyes like that on generals. Perhaps too much looking at death can kill a man's inside. It's not brave to refuse to back off from a mad dog; it's stupid. But with Andy I can't help myself. I have to push him. It is one thing to hear about an Andy Pappas and hate him, and another thing to really know an Andy Pappas and hate him. Part of it is fear, of course. I fear Andy as much as anyone else who really knows him, and that deepens the hate. I sit and talk to him, and I fear him and what he is capable of doing, and so I hate him more than anyone.

Another part is guilt. I feel guilty around Andy because, in some way, I have failed and he is my fault. I have to share the blame for Andy. I can't back off, tread softly as any man in his right mind should, because he is what is wrong with it all. A man like Andy Pappas is where we all went off the track. All the men like Andy who believe that all that counts is some advantage, some victory here and now no matter how it is done or who gets hurt. Any advantage, any victory. The men who will destroy us all just to win some small victory, if it is only to be King of the Graveyard.

'All right, Dan,' Pappas said at last. 'I'll make it short. Lay off Swede Olsen and his family.'

I won't say that it hit me between the eyes. It hit a lot lower than that. My stomach took an elevator ride, and all of it down. There was part of an answer to a lot of good questions. Somehow, Andy Pappas was involved in the Jo-Jo Olsen affair. It explained a great deal. If I were the Olsens I would be worried. If Andy Pappas had a stake in this, and I was on the wrong side, I would have done a rabbit—a very fast and far rabbit. I'm not the Olsens, I knew nothing, and I was still worried.

'Why?' I said.

'Olsen works for me,' Pappas said.

'Olsen?' I said. The question was clear.

Pappas shrugged. 'Not much. Odd jobs, driving, errands, stuff like that. But he gets my protection, Danny.'

'Does he need it, Andy?' I pushed.

Pappas laughed aloud. 'Look, Dan, I don't know it all. I don't even want to know it all. What I know is that Olsen doesn't want you bothering him or his family. Okay?'

'Did he tell you why I'm bothering him?'

Andy dried his hands fastidiously on the paper napkin that came with all drinks. 'I didn't talk to him. I got the request through channels, Dan. If it was anyone but you I'd have sent a punk to give the word.'

'His boy's done a rabbit,' I said.

'So it's a family matter. Since when do you work for the cops?'

'I'm not working for the cops. I'm working for a nice kid who wants to find his friend. A nice kid who was beaten ninety per cent to death today. I guess he didn't have the luck to have grown up with you, Andy.'

I got a flash of the claws and the terror of Andy Pappas.

'Back off, Dan!'

The dead eyes dilated with a flash of the essential insanity that must lurk deep inside Andy Pappas. Then they came back, and Andy smiled thinly.

'I don't beat ninety per cent, Danny.'

I pushed once more. 'Whose tail is getting burned, Andy? Who's been stepped on?'

It was the push of the absurd. Even Andy knew that I did not expect any kind of answer. He stood up, smiling.

'Remember, Danny, Olsen has my protection.'

When Pappas stands up it is a signal. The way when a king stands up it is a signal for everyone to rise. I heard the motor start in the big car up the block. Max Bagnio crossed the street towards us. Jake Roth stepped up to the table beside his boss. I found myself looking at Roth. His eyes were even shaped like the eyes of a snake. The snake eyes were fixed at me.

'He must be in real trouble, Andy,' I said to Pappas, but it was Jake Roth I was looking at.

It was Roth who answered me. The tall, skinny killer leaned half down and across that small table like a long-necked vulture. He stank of sweat in the heat. Roth never takes his coat off in public.

'Slow, peeper,' Roth said. 'Real slow. Mr Pappas said lay off. Mr Pappas said forget it. You never heard about no Olsen. You don't know the name. Mr Pappas said cool it. You cool it.'

Roth's black, luminous, snake-shaped eyes seemed to float in dark water. His breath was thick. He breathed fast as he bent his face close to me. Andy Pappas touched him lightly on the shoulder. Roth jerked upright like a dog on a leash.

'I told him, Jake,' Andy Pappas said. 'You can tell Olsen that Fortune got the word. Tell Swede it's okay.'

The black car purred up to the kerb. Pappas touched his dark blue homburg to Marty and climbed into the back of the car. Roth got in with Andy, and Little Max Bagnio went around and joined the driver in the front seat. The car eased away and turned into the Sixth Avenue traffic. I watched it go. I ordered a double Irish for both of us.

'I know that you know him,' Marty said, 'but I'm surprised every time. Just seeing him makes me shiver.'

'Join the club,' I said.

The drinks came.

'You know what is so terrible?' Marty said, her eyes still looking towards where the car had vanished. 'That a man like that, an animal like that, can actually affect people trying to live good, normal lives. I mean, he could help or harm me, my acting. An animal, a parasite like that.'

'Believe it,' I said.

'How can you talk to him like that?' Marty said, shivering.

'I can't talk to him any other way,' I said. 'What I never really understood is why he lets me. I guess even Andy needs to think he is human. I'm his human feeling, his charity.'

Marty shivered again. 'I wonder what trouble Olsen is in that he'd have to have Pappas' protection?'

'Who knows? Maybe it was Jo-Jo who killed Tani Jones. Maybe he knows who did.'

'Tani Jones?' Marty said, stared. 'My God, Dan, Pappas wouldn't protect anyone involved in her murder.'

She stared at me, I guess I stared back. I waited for her to drop the bomb I had guessed from her face.

'She was his girl friend, Dan. At the club, the girl who talked about her said she was Pappas' girl. I remember. This girl at the club said it was scary, the way Tani had loved jewels, and it was jewels that got her killed.'

I took a breath. 'Andy's married. A family man. He's real proud of being a family man.'

Marty laughed a female laugh. 'When did marriage or a family have much to do with a girl friend? Except to make it hard on the girl. I mean, I suppose that's why they kept it so quiet. He had to maintain his image—the devoted family man. This girl who knew her said they never met in public. He always came to her place. A hidden toy, you know?'

'Could she have been dangerous to him?'

'I don't know, Dan. The girl who knew her said she was pretty dumb. A real bird who loved the men. I don't think she really knew much about him, just that he was important. The girl who told us about her said that Tani seemed to think it was exciting to have a secret lover.'

But I had stopped listening. I was thinking about the killer of Andy Pappas' woman. I could imagine the fear of anyone who had killed Tani Jones, even in panic. I could imagine the problem of anyone who knew who had killed her.

I could imagine something else: men had killed their own mistresses for centuries.

CHAPTER 9

It was past quitting time, and outside in the evening streets of the city the people were hurrying home in the last bright summer sunlight as it faded into deep purple across the river above Jersey City. But Gazzo was in his office. Somehow he almost always is in his office, morning or evening. Perhaps because, as the captain himself says, it may be evening or morning out in the streets, but in his dim and silent office it is always midnight.

'Why the hell didn't you tell me Jones was Andy's girl?'

'You didn't ask, and it was none of your business,' the captain said. He looked very tired. Too tired to amuse himself with me. 'It still isn't your business, Dan.'

'It's even money he's after Jo-Jo Olsen,' I said. 'It's better than even he beat up my client.'

'No,' Gazzo said.

'Yes!' I said. 'It's a thousand-to-one Andy killed her, and Andy never liked a witness! Christ, Gazzo, who would dare kill Andy Pappas' girl friend?'

'No,' Gazzo said.

I swore. 'No, what?'

'No to everything,' the captain said. 'Pappas didn't kill her.'

'Alibi?' I said. 'Of course Andy would have an alibi. Andy would have the best alibi money could buy. Foolproof, airtight, beyond reproach.'

I was at that moment feeling bitter. Who else could kill Tani Jones? And Jo-Jo had seen enough to make him run very far. I would have run if I could place Andy Pappas on that street at the right time.

Gazzo slammed his hand flat on his desk. 'Knock it off!'

The captain glared at me. 'You think maybe I haven't been a cop long enough to know a real airtight alibi when I see one? Or maybe you think Pappas can buy me?'

Nobody can buy Gazzo. I know that more cops than I like to think about have their hands out for a fast buck every chance they can get, and I know they have found whole burglary rings actually run by policemen, but Gazzo cannot be bought. There are a lot of honest cops. Maybe it is only that Gazzo never needed extra money. Behind every five-dollar bill a patrolman takes there is a need, real or imagined. But that is another story.

'I'll listen,' I said.

Gazzo spelled it out for me. 'At the exact time of the burglary and killing, Andy Pappas was in Washington in front of that congressional committee investigating waterfront crime. If you had a brain, you'd have remembered that. If you think hard, you'll remember that the committee had been sweating Andy for three days solid. On the day of the killing he'd been on the stand all day; the session didn't end until eight o'clock that night. Even Andy can't turn time back.'

'He had it done,' I said. 'Sure, it's just the time he would pick. Were all his boys with him?'

'No, but they all have alibis.'

'Sure, probably each other.'

'No,' Gazzo said as if he were reading a very easy book to a dumb four-year-old. 'Jake Roth was at Pappas' place down on the Jersey shore. Pappas admits he had Jake out of sight and under wraps because Jake would make a lousy witness down in

Washington. Pappas had a sort of gentleman's agreement with the committee that he would show voluntarily if they wouldn't subpoena any of his boys. But Andy wasn't taking chances.'

'How about Max Bagnio?'

'Little Max was in Philadelphia on business. I didn't ask what business, but Pappas says he can trot out the witnesses if needed. They'll be hoods, but there'll be a lot of them. Most of the others were in Washington with Pappas or have alibis.'

'Airtight alibis?'

'Not like Pappas,' Gazzo said evenly. 'No one saw them who couldn't be bought, I admit that. Roth has the best. He was at Pappas' private beach all day. We checked that his car never left the shore. Bagnio was seen by enough reliable people in Philly, but it's a short trip up here. The rest can account for most of their time, but not all.'

'So none of them have real alibis,' I said.

'Who does, Dan?' Gazzo said. 'You've been around long enough to know that an alibi without an area of doubt hardly exists. Who can prove what he was doing every minute of a day unless he plans to do it or is lucky like Pappas. You know we have to go on probability. The boys all have alibis just good enough to make it hard for them to have killed the girl for Andy. Nothing is sure in this world.'

I swore again. 'It's got to be Pappas himself!'

I wanted it to be Andy. It's good to think that evil always trips itself up; that a deadly machine like Andy Pappas would be finally betrayed by his one weakness—that he was, after all, human enough to have a girl and be jealous. Only that was unlikely as the motive. With Andy it was more probable that the Jones girl had learned too much, that it was bad business to let her live—love or no love.

Gazzo sighed. 'Give me some credit, Dan, okay? Don't you think I want it to be Pappas? You think maybe I wouldn't like to nail him on this? My mouth waters when I think of it. I lie awake at night telling myself that this is just the kind of mistake that nails a guy like Pappas. Sure. Only I've been a cop too long to kid myself.'

'Meaning?'

'Meaning that I've got to be honest. I've got to go on what my experience and judgment tell me, and I know, as much as anyone can know anything, that Andy didn't kill her or have her killed.' Gazzo stopped and stared moodily into the shadows of his office. He picked a cigarette from his package and lighted it. His eyes were seeing something not easy to see. 'I was there when we told him, Dan. I mean, I wanted to be there. I was sure we had him. We didn't know about him until the maid told. We told him cold. I'm human, I wanted to see him squirm. Only I didn't like it when I saw his face.'

Gazzo smoked, looked at me. 'He almost fainted when we told him, Dan. I've told a lot of people about the death of someone they loved. I've seen a thousand faces when they get that news. I know what those faces look like, and I know a real shock and a real faint when I see one.'

The captain seemed to find the cigarette bitter to his taste. 'He cried, Dan. I mean, Andy Pappas really cried. You ever see Andy cry? Even when he was fifteen? I remember the day his old man was crushed to death on the docks. Andy just looked at what was left of the old man. This time he cried. He told me to get who killed her.'

'Touching,' I said.

But I wasn't as hard as I sounded. It was just, as I said, that I wanted Andy to make his mistake that way. I wanted Andy to get it from something as stupid, as simple, as human as a jealous rage;

some lousy little mistake anyone could have made. I wanted that real bad. Gazzo knew what I was thinking.

'I've been a cop a long time, Dan, and I know about Andy this time. Sure, we've checked it all ways and upside down, too. As far as we can learn, the girl was just a dumb kid who was proud to be Pappas' girl. Word says she never even knew exactly what Andy does. Everything says that Pappas was really hooked on the girl, treated her almost like a daughter.'

'Daughters cheat,' I said, 'and maybe she learned something she didn't even know she knew. Andy takes no chances.'

'Everything is possible, Dan,' Gazzo said, 'but we dug deep. There isn't a whisper against Pappas. It doesn't look like she even knew who he really was. They kept it pretty quiet, and she was like a toy to him. The worst you can say is she was dumb, and liked the men too much.'

'Maybe one man too many,' I said. 'Andy's human, maybe.'

'For God's sake, Dan, we're talking about Andy Pappas!' Gazzo roared at me. 'You think Andy would do such a lousy job of killing his own girl friend? You think he'd shoot her in her own apartment and just fake a burglary? You think he couldn't come up with a better cover than that?'

It was the best argument Gazzo had offered. Yes, I thought that Pappas would have done better. The girl had been closely tied to him. There would have been a more plausible 'accident'. And a sudden rage was out. Pappas had been in Washington. I did not see anyone else killing Pappas' sweetie on purpose. No, the burglar theory looked better now.

'That's why you weren't surprised that the loot hasn't turned up,' I said.

Gazzo nodded. 'Every fence in New York has those diamonds and pearls engraved on his brain. Pappas would see to that. To try to sell them would be a death warrant.'

A very quick death warrant. The question was: whose name was on that warrant? Someone was looking for Jo-Jo Olsen, and looking very hard. The next question was: Was it Pappas who was looking for Jo-Jo, or someone else? From the way Andy had acted when he warned me to lay off Swede Olsen and family, it did not seem that Andy was looking for Jo-Jo or had any idea that Jo-Jo might be connected to the death of Tani Jones. But Pappas is a clever man. He would not tip his hand, and he would not want me looking if he was looking. He could be playing both sides of the street—warning me off to lull Olsen, and looking for Jo-Jo himself. At least, whoever was looking was still looking. Which indicated that Jo-Jo was not yet in a shallow grave.

I left Gazzo to his perpetual midnight.

'Keep in touch,' the captain said. That, too, was an order.

On the hot streets it was almost night now. I could feel the city begin to move. New York is busy in the daylight, but it is at night that it really lives. You can feel the surge as the sun goes down across the river. It can be a wonderful moment, that night surge of the city, if you have something to do and somewhere to go. If you have nothing to do and nowhere to go it is a desolate moment. All I had to do for certain was chase down the Driscoll girl. It was too late for that, I had only an office address. After the Driscoll girl I was down to starting again looking for someone who knew anything about Jo-Jo, and checking the weary round of airline desks, train stations, and bus depots—something the police could do better, and that would lead to very little anyway. I was stymied.

But I had somewhere to go. Or I thought I did as I stood outside headquarters. Which proves how unclear my thinking was.

I wanted a drink and some company. I grabbed a taxi uptown for Monte's Kat Klub. I don't usually hang around the club. Marty is busy, and her job is to make the customers slobber over her three-quarters naked body; and she does a good job. On top of that the whiskey is cut and overpriced for the marks. But I wanted an ear, Marty can sometimes give me time between shows, and for me she can find a good bottle.

So I rode uptown and reached the club just in time for the first show. Or I almost reached the club. The cab could not get close, with the other cabs double-parked to let out the suckers. The driver had to drop me a block away.

I saw them. They were stationed casually on either side of the entrance to the club. Too casually. Not amateurs, maybe, but only semi-pros. They were not ridiculous in their stakeout, just bad enough for me to spot them and know them. Two average men in dark suits, one skinnier than the other. It was possible that they were waiting there for someone else. I knew better. Or, let's say I knew better than to take the chance. I walked in the other direction. If I had had any doubts I soon lost them. When I reached the corner of Macdougal Street I saw them coming behind me.

The crowds were moving in phalanxes up and down Macdougal. I had no desire to be caught in Washington Square Park, so I went south. I passed the San Remo and kept going south into the darker streets of Little Italy. They were still behind me. They looked eager. They seemed to enjoy their work. From their manner I guessed that they thought I had made a mistake by leaving the crowds and running down towards Houston Street. They were wrong. Danny the Pirate still had friends.

I went around the corner on Houston Street and broke into an instant sprint. I not only had friends, I knew the neighbourhood. They probably did too, but I was sure they thought they had me and that that would make them careless and too sure of themselves. I made it the three doors before the two came around behind me. I went down the dark flight of six stone steps like a man falling into a hole. At the bottom I knocked the signal, and the door opened. I slid through, and the door closed behind me.

'You got a wait for a seat, Fortune,' the steerer on the door said.

I went down the dark hall and into the room where the table sat green and decorated with money under its single overhead hanging lamp with the green metal shade. The cards were going around in a silence broken only by the cold voice of the dealer: '. . . ace for the johnnie, another blue, the ladies are paired, and here we go. You have a hunch, bet a bunch. Throw it in 'n it'll all come home. Ladies say they've got the hammer. The blue says no, could be a bucket, and bumps all the way. When you're out turn 'em over. Acey-Johnnie talks like three, 'n here we go . . .'

I knew the dealer, but he was in the slot and his cold eyes saw nothing but cards. My man was a shadow in a chair against the far wall. I had bought time, but not much. My two shadows would have turned the corner and found me gone. Maybe two, maybe three minutes of quick running, and then they would stop and they would know about the poker game down here. Maybe one minute. Any second I would hear the door open again far back down that long hall. I stepped to the shadow in the chair.

'Hello, Dan, some action? The shill in the jeans'll stand soon.'

'I need some time, Cellars,' I said. 'And the back door.'

'Cops?' Cellars Johnson said, tilting his chair forward until his black face came into view. 'Cellars' Johnson because he knew every cellar in Little Italy, the Village, and Chelsea where his poker game could be played.

'You know better,' I said. No man brought the cops after him into one of Cellars' games. It was not good manners.

Cellars stood up. I followed him back through the darkness. We reached the back door and Cellars unlocked it. I went through. I was in a back yard below street level. I went over a fence, across another yard, through an iron gate and up out on to Macdougal again.

The street was deserted. I ran back to Bleecker, across to Sixth Avenue, and flagged a taxi. Once in the cab I sat back. But I did not relax.

Now I was thinking clearly. Now I knew I had been wrong—I had nowhere to go. I knew nothing about Tani Jones or Stettin or Jo-Jo Olsen, but I was in this—and Andy Pappas was in it. With Pappas in it, and until I knew what it was all about, I could not go home. I could not go to Marty. They wanted to talk to me, and they would not let Marty or Joe just stand around watching. Until this was over, I had no friends. Not if I liked my friends. In that cab I never felt so alone in my life. Alone and scared.

I left the taxi in the heart of Chelsea and walked around a few blocks before I headed for the Manning Hotel. I took a room at the Manning. It is a cheap hotel about two notches above a flophouse, but they ask no questions and don't know my face. I took my key up to the room and locked myself in. The room was like a sweatbox, and the bed was hard and lumpy. The noise of the street came through the single open window with the blinking colours of the neon signs. There was no fire escape.

I stood at the window for some time and looked down on the street and the people in the neighbourhood I did not really belong to any more but that was reaching out to pull me back. I thought about all I had studied and learned and that it did not add up to enough to teach me to stay out of trouble. I wanted peace and no waves like everyone else, but I had listened to a kid who wanted to find his friend when by all the rules he should have minded his own business. Now I was in something that involved Andy Pappas, and there is no peace that way.

After a time I called Marty and Joe. I did not tell them where I was. I said I would be in touch. Then I sent down for a bottle of Irish and some ice and lay on the bed to think. What was I doing? I was looking for Jo-Jo Olsen. So was someone else. Who? There was a burglar, maybe. And a cop mugger, maybe. The burglar and the cop mugger could be the same man or they could be two different men. One or both could be looking for Jo-Jo. Or Pappas could be looking for Jo-Jo. Which could mean that Jo-Jo himself was either the burglar or the mugger.

Or it could mean that Pappas was the burglar and/or the mugger. (I did not rule out Pappas no matter what Gazzo said, and no matter how much I thought Gazzo was right.) I did not think Pappas was either killer or mugger, or that he had ordered one or both, but someone had hired my two shadows. I was sure that the shadows were hired. We live more and more in a faceless world. Everyone works for someone and does not care who he helps or who he kills. All that counts is his efficiency rating and his credit rating. As a matter of fact, it was not important at the moment who had done what, but only who was looking for Jo-Jo.

I took a long drink. If Pappas were looking for Jo-Jo he could be the killer, or think that Jo-Jo could tell him who the killer was, or think that Jo-Jo was the killer. If it was not Pappas who was looking, then it had to be either the burglar, the mugger, or someone I had not even learned about yet! I knew nothing about the mugger. I knew that the burglar had killed the woman of Andy Pappas, and that is enough to make a man run far and fast. It was also enough to make him hire men to find a witness. Except would a common burglar hang around to hire men, or have the power to hire men—especially to go up against Pappas?

I took another drink. If Jo-Jo knew who killed Tani Jones, why not tell Pappas at least? The Olsens were tight with Pappas. What reason would Jo-Jo have to protect a killer from Pappas? Or from the police? Okay, to not tell the police was the code, although Jo-Jo did not sound like a boy who respected the code, but to tip Pappas was not against the code, and it would get the tipster a medal. If Jo-Jo were the killer, okay, but I did not see Jo-Jo as the burglar-killer. Then who was Jo-Jo protecting? If he was protecting anyone. If he knew anything. I took a big drink.

Because it was all still nothing. Not a shred of actual proof of anything. All I had were unconnected crimes and facts, and a missing boy I was trying to find. Nothing more, except that someone else was also looking, for reasons unknown to me. I really knew nothing.

No one was going to believe that. And there was my problem.

I had asked questions. I seemed to be involved, and it is not what you are that counts, it is what you seem to be. It isn't reality that matters, it is what people think is real and act on. Not what is true, but what people believe is true.

So I was alone in a cheap hotel room. I was drinking alone and sweating alone. I was on a lumpy bed in a dark room in a world where I did not belong. A world that was pulling me back because I was looking for a missing boy. A world I could die in if I did not find that boy soon.

CHAPTER 10

I woke up with a hangover and a knot in my stomach. I had not slept well. I had dreamed of running alone down a long dark street chasing my missing arm as it floated ahead of me just out of reach. I had a drink. I had two drinks until the knot in my gut eased and my hands stopped sweating. Then I got up and dressed and slipped out and down the back way. Because I had to do something more than hide in a cheap room.

The Trafalgar Travel Bureau was on the second floor of a big midtown building. I was camped outside the door when the staff began to arrive. The first to show was a middle-aged lady, grey and belligerent. She unlocked, and I followed her inside. She asked if she could help me. I told her I wanted the manager. I looked as dangerous as I could. (I look more dangerous than I am after a bad night.) She considered my missing arm and retreated. She vanished somewhere, but I sensed her watching me.

Four more females arrived in due time. They came in order of good looks, the best-looking last, which gave me some idea of what the boss was like. I mean, an office worker in New York will take every liberty he or she can get away with, and in this office it looked like the prettier the girl the more she could get away with. This did not surprise me. Each girl gave me the eyes up-and-down as she came in, and then looked at the grey one, who shrugged.

My man arrived promptly at nine forty-five. I figured he ran a loose ship.

'You the manager?' I asked, trying to sound official.

'Walsh,' he said. I'm the manager. What . . .'

'It's private,' I said.

He hesitated, then nodded. 'Okay, come on in.'

His office was nothing to brag about, but it was private and it had four windows. He took his time about getting settled and asking me to sit down. I saw the pictures of his wife and kids, three, on his desk and a pretty good-sized cabin cruiser beside them. The picture of the boat was better framed than the picture of his wife. He waved me to a seat, and the telephone rang. While he answered I had a good look at him. He was tall, handsome, in a seedy way, and well dressed. His face was heavily tanned, which helped him a lot. It tended to hide the bald spot on his skull and gave him an athletic appearance. His face was thin, he wore a pencil moustache, grey now, and he had a habit of rubbing his bicep with his free hand. He seemed to be feeling his own muscle.

'So,' he said when he hung up, 'what can I do for you, Mr . . .?'

'Dan Fortune. You can tell me where I can find Miss Driscoll.'

'Nancy—?'

His voice gave him away when he tried to stop. The 'Nan' part of Nancy came out fast and surprised. The end of the name was modulated and trailed off. His jaw muscles clamped hard to prevent any more involuntary sounds. I could see the knots of muscle along his jaw. I had also seen the surprise. The name had hit him unprepared. Exactly why it was a shock I didn't know, but I could guess. Judging from the way he ran his office, Mr Walsh liked young ladies. But I was not interested in the manager's love life unless it related to Jo-Jo Olsen.

'Miss Nancy Driscoll, right,' I said as if remembering some official report that had sent me here to the travel bureau. 'I'd like to talk to her.'

'I'm afraid she's not here,' Walsh said.

There was a tone in his voice that started a small alarm in my brain. Walsh was being cautious. And something else. The manager had a faint question in his voice. The caution could be caused by his interest in the girl, if he had an interest. But what was the question I heard?

'When do you expect her?' I said. I decided to be cautious too.

'I, ah, couldn't say, Mr Fortune,' Walsh said. 'May I ask what your interest is?'

'I can't say,' I said as brusquely as I could, trying to sound like a policeman. 'But I have to talk to her. Maybe you can tell me where she is.'

Walsh squeezed at the bicep muscle of his left arm with his right hand. 'Well, I'm not sure . . .'

I had a thought. 'How long since she's been to work, Mr Walsh?'

'What?' the manager said. 'Oh, well, about a week. Yes, this is Friday, and she hasn't been in since last Friday. I mean, she was here all day last Friday, but not since.'

'In other words, she didn't show last Monday and hasn't been in all week.'

'Yes,' Walsh said. 'That's it.'

'Has she called in?'

'Er, well, no,' Walsh said.

There it was again. The caution and question in the voice of the manager. Did he think I was a snooper hired by his wife? That was more than possible. He was nervous about something. I began to think that the manager had more than a passing interest in Nancy Driscoll. He was acting very much like a man with a lot on his mind and a hot potato in his pocket. But just at that moment I had more on my mind than an office scandal.

The Driscoll girl had not been to work all week. She had not called in sick, if Walsh were telling the truth. And Jo-Jo had done his fadeout last Friday. I felt a lot like swearing. After all I had done so far it could turn out that Jo-Jo Olsen was just off with the Driscoll girl. There could be a hundred reasons why he would not tell about it. No, there had to be more. My two shadows were looking for Jo-Jo for some reason. Still, it was possible that Jo-Jo had planned to run far and stay long and had taken the Driscoll girl along.

'All right,' I said, 'suppose you give me her address.'

'Well, I . . .' Walsh began.

'I think you'd better,' I said.

Walsh considered me. 'She lives at 145 West Seventy-Fourth Street, apartment 2B.'

'Thanks,' I said.

All the females watched me go. The grey-haired harpie gave me a smug look as if she was sure that her Mr Walsh had handled my type. I grinned all around, and they became busy. I glanced back. Walsh had forgotten to close his door behind me. I saw him through the open door. He was talking fast on the telephone. I had not heard it ring. Walsh was calling someone. I had a good hunch that it was about me.

All at once another possibility occurred to me. I did not like the thought. Maybe my two shadows and the mayhem so far on Pete had no connection to Stettin or Tani Jones but to Nancy Driscoll. It was possible. Maybe Jo-Jo had run off with the Driscoll girl and someone did not like that. My two hard types could be looking for Jo-Jo about Nancy Driscoll. It was as good a theory as any other I had come up with. With the little I knew, it was a fine theory.

It was also a dangerous theory. If it had any germ of truth in it, Walsh was probably calling down the wolves on me.

I got out of that office and out of the building. Once I reached the crowded midtown street I felt better. Somehow daylight and sun and crowds make a man feel safer. What can happen in broad daylight on a street full of innocent people? Plenty, that's what can happen. I can name six unsolved killings that took place in broad daylight on a city street. Caution was indicated.

So I took the short subway ride up to Seventy-second Street, with a careful and watchful change at Columbus Circle, and went warily up out of the station into the heat.

I walked north on Central Park West in the shadow of the Dakota Apartments. The park was across the street to the right. It was still early and the park was green and bright in the sun. New York, in summer, is always at its best before eleven o'clock in the morning. The air is clearer then, the heat not yet an oven.

I turned left down Seventy-Fourth Street. It was a street of nursing homes and renovated brownstones. As I reached Columbus Avenue I began to watch all round. I was wary. Crowds can be a help when you want to hide or fade away, but they can also hide men looking for you. Columbus Avenue was crowded. The one-way traffic thundered down with the staggered lights like a massive herd of roaring animals. I crossed on the green, and approached 145 on the far side of the street.

This block between Columbus and Amsterdam Avenues was far different. It was a polyglot mess of rooming-house brownstones, old and shabby brown-stones, renovated brownstones, refaced brownstones, and a few tall modern apartment houses. There was also a school and a cheap hotel at the Amsterdam Avenue corner. I passed 145 across the street and walked casually on to the corner. But I had had a good look at 145.

It was a renovated pair of brownstones combined into one apartment house but still with two entrances. I knew that 2B would be the parlour floor rear—about the best apartment in the building. With two apartments on the floor, it would be a small apartment. I waited for a time at the corner. I saw no one who seemed interested in me and no one suspicious. I had come to talk to Miss Nancy Driscoll. I walked back to 145 on its side of the street, and went down into the vestibule.

It was a small vestibule. The kind with an outer and inner glass door, coloured tiles on the floor, and the row of mailboxes between the two doors. There was no mail in Nancy Driscoll's mailbox, which could mean that she had not gone away, or had come back. It could also indicate that she did not get much mail. I pressed the bell of 2B and waited. In the tiny vestibule I was feeling as exposed and nervous as a fish in a fishbowl. There was no one on the street outside who looked suspicious or dangerous, but I had that tingling in the arm that wasn't there that comes when I sense that all is not right. The door buzzed and I pushed it open and went in. It was a good sign. Nancy Driscoll was at home. I needed some good signs about now.

The cellar door was directly in front of me at the end of a short hall. There was no elevator. I checked the cellar door and found it open. That was a good thing to know, just in case. Inside, it was a typical West Side apartment house, the hall and stairwell empty and silent with everyone out at work in the morning. I went up the stairs slowly. There was one short flight, a landing, another short flight, and the first floor. The first floor turned out to be no more than a small landing with two doors at right angles and the stairs going on up. The door to 2B was directly in front of me. I listened but heard no sound inside. I pressed the doorbell.

The door opened instantly.

A man stood there.

There was a pistol in his right hand.

I tried for the stairs down.

'Don't try!'

I stopped.

'Inside.'

I turned and walked into the apartment. The man followed me down the narrow kitchen, the pistol steady in his hand, and into the living-room, which had a fine old fire-place and high ceiling. One look told me that Nancy Driscoll, wherever she was, had been a girl who wanted things—Things, you understand? The living room was filled with all the proper pieces of furniture: a small bar stocked with all the proper glasses, the whiskey in decanters with little metal name tags; there were the proper candle-sticks, bric-á-brac, prints on the walls; the bookcases were filled with elegant sets that looked as if they had never been cut and rows of best-sellers jacketed in plastic. Nancy Driscoll was a girl who wanted what everyone else in the middle had or wanted.

'Against the wall! Hands flat on the wall. Lean.'

I leaned against the wall with my lone hand flat on it. I felt his hand give me a quick but complete frisk for weapons. I came up clean, and he stepped back.

'Okay, sit down.'

I sat on a cheap modern couch facing him. Up close, the couch and everything else in the apartment was cheap, shoddy, built to look elegant but made of boxwood, pegboard and tacks. And I guessed that Nancy Driscoll had spent most of her salary for a lot of years to get together this pitiful show of what she yearned to have but could have only in shoddy imitation. I was getting a picture of Nancy Driscoll. A sad picture.

My captor put his pistol away in a small belt holster.

'Who are you? What do you want with the Driscoll dame?'

He was a man of medium height and weight. His suit was old and had not cost more than fifty dollars new. His shoes were worn and half-soled. His hat had not been blocked for years. His socks drooped. His face was pale and tired. I looked at him and knew who Walsh had called. A man who looked and acted like this man and who had the right to carry a gun could only be a policeman. The cheapest hood would not have been so poorly dressed or so tired. He had detective written all over him, and he had been waiting for me.

'Fortune,' I said. 'Walsh tipped you, right? I'm a private operator.'

'Good for you,' the man said. 'Now tell me about the Driscoll woman.'

'A case,' I said. 'The trail led here. Call Captain Gazzo at Homicide if you want to check, Lieutenant . . .?'

'Sergeant Doucette,' he said. 'The girl wasn't very important, Fortune.'

I heard the word. 'Wasn't?'

'Yeh, she's dead. I figured you could . . .'

The sergeant stopped and shrugged. I knew how he felt. He needed a break. I felt worse. I seemed to be moving fast backwards. Every lead turned into a new crime, and I was no closer to Jo-Jo Olsen. Except that this time I knew that Jo-Jo was connected to the Driscoll woman, and I now had a real reason for a man to run. It was not a happy thought.

'When?' I said.

'I thought you could tell me,' Sergeant Doucette said. 'I guess we better go talk to the lieutenant.'

'I'd rather talk to Captain Gazzo.'

Doucette shrugged again. 'From here you go to the lieutenant. After that he'll tell you.'

He walked behind me out of the apartment and down the stairs. I decided that Doucette had been a detective long enough. He believed nothing and no one. He took no chances. In his work that was a good rule.

Gazzo clasped his hands behind his head and looked up at the ceiling of his office. I sat and smoked. The captain again did not look as if he had slept. But then, he always looked like that. Why would a man bother to sleep when the clock in his brain never moved from midnight and it was hard to tell if the faces that passed before him were real or in a dream?

'This is getting to be a habit,' the captain said. 'A bad penny. Nobody likes bad pennies. You sure there is a Jo-Jo Olsen?'

There was a faint edge to Gazzo's voice. I knew that it did not mean anything. It was a reflex. I was not a visitor this time. I was a man picked up looking for a murder victim, at the scene of the crime, and the captain's voice automatically took on the hard edge, the hint of suspicion. Gazzo could not help it, the way an old fighter cannot resist a bell.

'How did the Driscoll girl die?' I asked. 'The lieutenant forgot to tell me.'

I was beginning to feel like a puppet on a string. No matter what I did I ended up asking questions like a straight man in a nightclub routine. All my efforts so far had only uncovered more possible mayhem to lay at Jo-Jo Olsen's door.

'Multiple bruises and contusions that led to fatal brain damage,' Gazzo said. 'In other words she was knocked around by someone with heavy hands.'

'There seems a lot of knocking around in this,' I said.

Gazzo was thoughtful. 'No robbery, no forcible entry.'

'When?'

'Sometime last Saturday, the M.E. says. We found her on Monday. That manager, Walsh, found her. When she didn't show for work he called her. He got no answer so went around. At least, that's his story. He had a key.'

Now I knew what had been strange about Walsh. I also heard the first solid motive for murder and runout in this whole mess. One woman, two men. Classic. Only it had been the Driscoll girl after Jo-Jo, according to my reports, which made the motive fit Walsh a lot better than Jo-Jo.

'Is Walsh clear?'

The captain stared at his ceiling. 'Who's ever clear? He was at home with his family in Port Washington on Friday night. Early Saturday he took his boat out alone. He was out all day. Says he was cruising eastward on the sound. No one saw him he can be sure of. Stayed overnight on the boat somewhere near Port Jefferson and got home about noon on Sunday.'

'He could have cruised west into the river,' I said. 'There's a marina at about Seventy-ninth Street.'

'That there is. He didn't dock there, not officially.'

'Nothing to stop him dropping anchor near shore.'

'Nothing at all.'

'How come it took so long to discover the body?'

'Miss Driscoll was an oddball. A lot of men, but no real friends. There's one girl friend, a Peggy Brandt, who lives a few blocks away. The Brandt girl tells us that Driscoll had a yen for men, so no one was surprised if she did not answer her phone on a week-end. On top of that, the Brandt girl says she called Driscoll on Saturday afternoon and got the impression that a man was already there, so didn't call back.'

'Saturday afternoon?' I said. Jo-Jo had gone on Friday. Or had he? He had left Chelsea, but had he left the city?

'How does Olsen fit in this one?' Gazzo said.

I explained the various leads to Driscoll. 'Petey seemed to think she could know something. He wasn't sure. The picture I get is that the girl was trying to marry Jo-Jo.' I thought about it all. Pete had pretty much said that he thought Driscoll might know something. 'Maybe someone else followed the same trail I did, Captain. Maybe they asked questions too hard.'

'It has the look,' Gazzo conceded. 'Only someone was with her on Saturday who she knew. Guys have played hard to get before and then turned around and killed when the dame looked elsewhere.'

I had thought of that one minute after I ran into Sergeant Doucette. 'How come you didn't make Jo-Jo in this before me?'

Gazzo rubbed his stubble. 'No names. We couldn't find any address book or notes in her place. The Brandt girl says she never did hear the last names of most of Driscoll's men, except Walsh. It seems that Driscoll was chasing a couple of guys with a ring in mind, but that they were ducking, so she took up with Walsh. Walsh had been after her for a while.'

'No address book?'

'Maybe she didn't keep one,' Gazzo said.

Gazzo did not believe that either. Who would steal her address book? Some guy who wanted his name out of it. Or maybe two hoods looking for clues to where a boy was?

'I like Walsh for a killer,' I said.

'So do I, but the book says I need some proof.'

'How about the two who beat up Vitanza? It's the pattern, and she knew Olsen.'

'I've got an open mind,' Gazzo said.

'But you like Jo-Jo best?'

The captain sighed. 'I've got to like him. Motive, opportunity, and he's on the run. You know that's how it works most of the time. They hit, scare, and run. Maybe there's even more to it, but it looks like he stopped on his way and belted the Driscoll girl out.'

'Just because he's on the run?'

'That's a good start, but I've got this too.'

The captain held up a tiny miniature red racing car. Even from where I sat I could see that it was almost perfect in detail. There was a loop at the rear end. The loop was broken. The car was battered and scratched as if carried in a pocket a long time. It looked like a Ferrari.

'You said Olsen was a bug on racing,' Gazzo said.

'Especially on Ferraris,' I said.

I looked at that miniature racing car. It was obviously some kind of good-luck piece. A charm, a talisman. Some luck.

'It was under her body,' Gazzo said. 'There was also a handkerchief with bloodstains on it—and grease. Looks like he wiped her face before he knew she was dead. The handkerchief is too common to trace. A lot of cigarette butts. An empty bourbon bottle, wiped clean. Beer cans, also wiped.'

Jo-Jo had run. Jo-Jo was a fanatic on racing cars. Jo-Jo worked around a grease pit. Bottles and beer cans did not sound like two hoods asking questions. The address book, if there had been one, was missing. That sounded like someone who knew Driscoll.

Gazzo sighed. 'It fits, Dan. I had no lead to Olsen, it happened way out of his neighbourhood.'

'But I brought him to you,' I said.

'You're helping him a lot,' Gazzo said.

I was really helping Jo-Jo. So far I had helped tie him potentially to a murder close to home and definitely tied him to a murder victim a long way from home. I was doing fine.

'I've changed the pickup on Olsen to suspected of murder,' the captain said.

CHAPTER 11

You go on the probable in this world, I've said that before. Captain Gazzo was going on the probable of what he had. From where the captain sat, it was logically Jo-Jo. But I had another seat and another factor. I had the character of Jo-Jo Olsen as it had been emerging as I went along, and in my book Jo-Jo Olsen was not probable.

It can be misleading to talk only to a man's friends or a man's enemies, but no matter how I sliced the pie it still came out that Jo-Jo Olsen was not a violent type. Nothing made it probable that Jo-Jo Olsen would lose his temper over a woman. Possible of course—anything is possible—but not probable. The way it came out in my mind was that Jo-Jo might lose his temper over a racing car, but not much else. Even if he did, his reaction would not be violent.

And violence was the key.

I stood in the afternoon heat and sun of the city outside police headquarters and looked at the whole picture, and it was all violence. The quick and efficient violence against Patrolman Stettin. The unplanned violence of the burglar that had killed Tani Jones. The calculated violence for a purpose that had put Pete Vitanza into the hospital. The peripheral violence of Swede Olsen. The menace of violence that were my two shadows. The infinite potential of violence that was Andy Pappas. The animal violence of a Jake Roth or Max Bagnio under Pappas' orders. Naked violence from end to end. I could not place Jo-Jo Olsen into that picture.

But the only one connected to Nancy Driscoll was Jo-Jo.

If my logic was to be more than wishful thinking, I needed a connection between the Driscoll girl and some other factor in the affair; or I had to rule her out of the case by labelling an outsider as her killer, someone who had no other connection to Jo-Jo Olsen or anyone else in this affair. Someone like Walsh. If someone outside all the other problems had killed Nancy Driscoll, then there would still be no concrete connection of Jo-Jo to any specific crime. I would be no worse off. If I could bring someone I already knew into a connection with Driscoll, I could be better off.

There was only one place to go for an answer—the people who had known Nancy Driscoll. Maybe the police had missed something. They do miss something sometimes, although not really very often. But this time they had been asking without knowledge of Jo-Jo. I went back into headquarters and up to Gazzo's office. I got the addresses of the Brandt woman from the captain's pretty sergeant, on Gazzo's okay. I went back into the heat and hailed a cab. I had two addresses for the Brandt girl. I gave the office address, since it was only afternoon, and sat back with the window open and let the wind blow against my face and tried to think of nothing.

It did not work. It never does. My mind whispered around and around the same point—I was missing the key. I tried to think of Marty. That wasn't hard. She was easy to think about. But my mind saw her as if in a silent movie, her body and her face moving, but the offstage voice whispering that there was a key to all this, and that I should have seen the key by now. One small, out-of-normal incident gnawed like a worm in my brain. I could not place it. And there were a host of larger hints. They talked to me, but they did not say anything. My mind was not receiving. I forced myself to think of anything.

The wind, I thought of the wind on my face in the oven of tall buildings and crowded people that was midtown New York. It was a strong, hot wind as the taxi moved as fast as it could. Like the sirocco that had blown through a room I had tried to sleep in once near Palermo. Or the wind from the desert on a stopover I had made in Libya. There is a sobering sense of mortality in thinking about places you have been, strangers you have lived among. All things pass, and you will pass with them. There is a sadness in it, and without sadness there is no sense of life. Life is limited, and there is all the good and most of the bad. Life is arrival, departure and change, and those who never move do not live.

The taxi driver had to turn around and tell me that we were at my address. I paid him and got out. Miss Peggy Brandt worked in the Union Carbide Building. It towered tall and glass and steel, high above Park Avenue. I went into the lower lobby and rode the escalator up to the real lobby and the elevators. I read the directory and took an express elevator to the thirty-second floor. Miss Brandt worked inside expanses of glass, chrome, leather, carpets four-inches deep, and the brittle smile of a blonde receptionist. The gorgeous guardian of the gate made me cool my heels. Miss Brandt appeared, and her face took on a shell the instant she saw me. Her eyes flickered to my empty coat sleeve. She was tall, pretty, and calm. I explained my business. She led me down a soundless hall, deep in carpet, to an empty conference room.

'What do you do here, Miss Brandt?' I asked. I was interested. It was a trick to keep her friendly, but I was interested, too. I have always been interested in women who are in the struggle between the womb and the brain. In some ways it is the war of our time, for women at least, and a lot of the time for the men too. If a woman wants only one or the other, there is no trouble—for man or woman. But if she tries for both, then the war is on, and there is a price to pay for her and for the man.

'I'm an editor,' she said. 'I've already told the police all I know, Mr Fortune.'

'Sure,' I said. 'I just wanted a better picture of Nancy. I'm looking for a murderer, and I have to know who was murdered.'

Peggy Brandt crossed her very nice legs. She arched her back. Her breasts thrust out. I took it all in. She was not interested in me, I was much too old for the male she had in mind, but she automatically put herself on display, showed the wares, as women who still want to be the female chosen by the male always do. They were good wares.

'I've tried to think,' Peggy Brandt said, 'but it's hard. Nancy was a strange girl. No, she wasn't strange, she was too damned usual. Have you seen her apartment?'

I nodded. Peggy Brandt saw that apartment in her mind.

'She had to have it all: the furniture, the prints, the proper place,' the girl said. 'Time was passing, you understand? She had seen too many movies about bright young married people. She read the women's magazines and dreamed about living that fine, suburban life.' There was an edge of scathing contempt in Peggy Brandt's voice, mixed with a faint regret. She was in the war all right. Inside she must have looked like a battleground of maimed desires. 'She was a poor girl, from a poor family out in Queens. Corona, I think. Semiskilled workers: beer and bowling, eat at the kitchen table, wear undershirts and make love in the back seat of the car. She had no skills, no career or desire for a career. She couldn't afford the things she considered she had to have, so bought cheap imitations. The men she knew were all wrong; men like her father and brothers. When she found a man she thought would be right he never seemed to want to marry right away. The only men she met and wanted were men who had come from the same background but were fighting to get out and had ambitions and did not want to marry yet.'

'Like Jo-Jo Olsen?' I said.

'Jo-Jo?' the girl shook her pretty head. 'I don't know any Jo-Jo. I guess you mean this Joseph. I never knew his last name. Nancy did not talk much. I knew she had a man named Joe, younger than she. She liked him a lot, I think. You never could really tell with Nancy. I mean, the man himself wasn't as important as the picture she had of the man and herself in a cosy marriage nest. But I think she liked him, at least she thought he was the man who could give her the life she wanted. I got the impression that he was in no hurry. She was. I never saw a girl in so much hurry.'

I listened. Whenever we talk about someone else we are really also talking about ourselves. If you listen closely enough to what a person says about someone else, you can get a pretty good picture of what that person thinks of himself, what view of life the speaker has. Peggy Brandt was talking about Nancy Driscoll and what the Driscoll girl had wanted, but she was really considering what she, Peggy Brandt, wanted. She was wondering if she was in a hurry, or if she should be in more of a hurry. If, perhaps, she wasn't missing something, if her career was, after all, that important.

'Jo-Jo was in no hurry,' I said, prompted. 'He had ambitions. He was going to be a racing driver.'

'Yes, Joseph liked cars,' Peggy said. 'Nancy used to tell me how they would live all over the world. But she couldn't get him to marry her, I suppose. Anyway, she started dating almost anyone. She was something of a tease, I think. Girls who have only marriage on their minds often are. I don't think they mean to tease, but they just don't understand that love and marriage do not always go together to all people. Nancy told me of a few nasty scenes with the men she started dating.'

'Any names?' I broke in. 'Someone who might . . .'

'No, I told the police I never knew their names. She was bitter about this Joseph, and every day she seemed to get more anxious about getting old and not yet married to the right man to give her the good life. She did foolish things, from the little she told me. I got the impression she was trying with every man she met.' The Brandt girl stopped. She uncrossed and recrossed her fine legs, absently rubbed her thigh. She was thinking about every man she met. 'Then there was Walsh.'

'She was his mistress?'

The Brandt girl nodded. 'She told me. Walsh had been after her for a long time. I don't know, Mr Fortune, I think she sort of snapped. Inside, you know? She was in such a hurry. The men she knew were so nothing. Young boys who could give her little and did not want to marry. Walsh couldn't marry, but he could give her something. One day she just took it, said yes to him. She said she was tired of waiting.' She looked straight at me. 'It's illogical, Mr Fortune, but there is a type of woman who won't let a potential husband touch her before he makes it marriage, but will sleep, at last, with a man who cannot even think of marriage.'

'I know,' I said.

It was an old and sad story. A nice and proper young virgin who is lonely, anxious, in a hurry. She wants not a man but marriage—and she wants a man, too. She is bored, feels empty, cheated. Somehow she cannot make love to a man who might marry her before they are married. It's a block in her. Then she meets a man who cannot marry her, who only wants her for sex and adventure, and all her desires come out without the check of possible marriage. It becomes a paradox. She has an impregnable barrier deep inside against passion without marriage, and it takes a strange twist because suddenly marriage does not exist, cannot happen, and the need becomes naked without the barrier. Her barrier is against passion before marriage. Without the potential of marriage, suddenly there is only passion.

'Do you think Walsh killed her?' I said.

'I don't know, Mr Fortune. Who knows what happened between them? He came to her apartment. She went on trips on his boat. She even went on business trips with him sometimes. It was strange, but the way she talked about Walsh I had the feeling that she separated her life with him from her pursuit of a husband. A man might not understand that.'

'No,' I said. 'Can you tell me anything more about that Saturday?'

'Nothing,' she said 'A girl like Nancy doesn't confide much. She lives in a kind of dream world. Every male was a goal, every female a rival.'

'What about a woman?' I said. 'As the killer?'

'I think I'm about the only woman she knew.'

'Mrs Walsh?'

'I wouldn't know, Mr. Fortune.'

She stood up and looked at her watch. 'I have work, I'm sorry.'

I left. I had learned nothing that harmed Jo-Jo Olsen, and nothing that helped him, unless you counted the fact that it did not sound like there was a motive for Jo-Jo. The girl had been after him. Gazzo had not indicated that the girl had been pregnant. It was the kind of killing where the motive and the killer would be discovered at the same time. Sooner or later, one of the men Nancy Driscoll had known would be found without an alibi, with motive and opportunity, and he would be the man. It would take only time. Such cases were the commonplace of police work.

Somewhere in the city, or in some other city by this time, a man sweated in a bar and tried to think he would not be caught and tried to remember why he had lost his head and killed a woman he thought he was in love with. He had not been caught yet only because it was amazing how little any of us really know of the lives of our friends when they are not with us. Time, that was all, and the slow routine of the police.

Unless this was one of those one-in-a-thousand killings that was not simple, that tied in with more and bigger crime.

On the chance, I would try Walsh again.

I walked from Park Avenue west to the office of the Trafalgar Travel Bureau. Walsh was not glad to see me. He could tell by my face that I knew more than when I had been in his office this morning. He was nervous. He hurried me into his office as if he felt that all the women in his office were watching him. They were. I guessed that he had had a shot at most of them who he thought would look good in a nightgown and that he knew they all knew about Nancy Driscoll. He was a confused man. He was proud of his conquest of Nancy Driscoll, but terrified of discovery by the wrong people. A nervous lover can be dangerous.

'I'm sorry about calling the police, Mr Fortune, but . . .' Walsh began. He was rubbing his bicep.

'You thought I was a killer,' I said. 'Yes, you did! What happened, Walsh, was she going to blow the whistle?'

Under his tan Walsh was ashen. 'No! She . . . she loved me.'

'You don't believe that,' I said. 'She was bored, she wanted a sugar-baby. How much did she cost you a month?'

Walsh smirked at me. He rubbed at his bald spot. 'You're way off, Fortune.'

I noted the disappearance of the 'mister'. Walsh was being man-to-man, virile.

'All she wanted was me. I'm pretty good, if you want to know.'

'I'll dream about you,' I said.

He flushed under that fine tan, but his eyes snapped as if in memory of his own prowess. That was what pleased him, his own prowess, not the pleasure of a woman. He was probably pretty good, ego-maniacs often are.

'I gave her what she wanted, and it wasn't money.'

'You gave her what she wanted plus money, if I know women and your kind, Walsh,' I said.

He flexed his muscles. 'I gave her some stuff. Why not?'

'Ask your wife.'

Walsh leaned forward. 'Leave her out.'

'What happened? Did Nancy tell you she was running off with Joe?'

'Joe?'

'The guy she wanted to marry.'

'Him? Not unless he changed his mind. Him and his racing cars. Jesus! Can you imagine a guy who'd prefer a motor to the action Nancy could give? These kids, Jesus! She told me once that all they talked about when they came up to her place was racing.' He smirked again. 'I didn't talk about racing.'

'You knew Jo-Jo?'

'Who?'

'Joseph, her boyfriend.'

'I knew of him, Fortune, no more. Do you think he killed her? Maybe he found out about me and couldn't take it after all.'

It was a good shot. The thought had occurred to me more than once by now. It had, of course, also occurred to Gazzo. It happened; men are like that. It's called dog in the manger, and it's as good a reason for a beating as any; and maybe Walsh was so good in bed the Driscoll girl had been hooked on him. And maybe Jo-Jo had been on the run already and, with his dreams shattered, had changed his mind and tried to take Nancy with him. A sudden shift of power can destroy a man. But I did not want Walsh to get the impression that he had shaken my ideas.

'I think you killed her,' I said.

I thought he was going to come over the desk. I braced and looked for a weapon. But he changed his mind and sat back and just watched me.

'Did your wife worry you?' I said. 'Did Nancy get ideas?'

'The police don't think I killed her.'

'They can change their mind.'

'Not with my alibi.'

'You've got no alibi. Anyone can turn a boat in the other direction.'

'You have to prove it.'

'I may try,' I said. 'I may do a little snooping around. I may even do a lot of snooping.'

Now he was scared, really scared, but it was not of what I might find.

He leaned at me. 'You stay away from me! You hear? I don't want you around my life! I don't want . . .'

'I don't care what you want, Walsh,' I said.

He sweated in that good cool office with its big desk and four windows. He changed his tactics from bluster to man-to-man comradeship. 'Come on, Fortune, give me a break. If my wife . . . my kids . . .'

What he was afraid of was his wife finding out—now. I mean, after all, why get caught now that he couldn't get any use out of Nancy Driscoll?

'I don't care about you, Walsh,' I said. 'How about Nancy?'

He wiped at his face with a Kleenex from a monogrammed leather box. I don't know anything. I called her on the Saturday.

All right, I didn't tell the police that. Why should I? I'm not involved really, and if my wife . . .'

'You called her,' I said.

'She had this man with her. She was mad, said he was drunk, a rotten drunk kid. She said all men were cheats. This guy was there, you know? I mean, listen, Fortune, give me a break. Lay off my wife, my home. I mean . . . please?'

I got out of there. Maybe he killed her, and maybe not. (I was sure he had not killed her. His story checked the Brandt girl's story.) But if he had done it, Gazzo would nail him. It looked like Gazzo was playing it soft, maybe to lull Walsh, or maybe to spare three kids who had hurt no one yet. But if Jo-Jo did not pay off, Walsh was in for a bad time. Walsh did not have a rosy future. That did not make me sad.

I needed something clean. There was only Marty. I called her from the lobby of the building. She was at home. When I heard her voice I had to see her. I had to. I had not seen my shadows all day. Maybe I could chance it. I had to see her if I died for it.

Which is an easy thing to say.

CHAPTER 12

'You can't catch what you can't see,' I said. 'That's called philosophy. I got that from the manager of some baseball team. His centrefielder had just dropped two fly balls.'

Marty was in her street clothes now. The apartment was cool with her air-conditioning. The bedroom was dark, the shades drawn over the closed windows and the night outside. I had drawn the shades partly out of propriety and partly in case my two shadows made a return appearance. So far they had not. The last time I had looked, the street had held no menace. I had not looked for some time, and I had finished my third beer while Marty dressed. She does not hide when she dresses or undresses. She knows that there is beauty in the simple fact of a proud and matter-of-course nakedness. She understands that it is important that there be as few hidden and private corners between a man and a woman as possible. It must be as complete and simple as possible, and after the love it is important to lie side by side and smoke, to talk easily, to finally get up and dress quietly together.

Now I had my fourth beer and lay dressed on the bed while she sat in the bedroom chair. It was almost time for her to leave for work.

'It's easier to face something when you know what it is,' Marty said.

'No,' I said, 'its not easier at all, but it's better. If I knew what it was I'd probably be more scared than I am, but I'd feel better about it.'

'It's a mess, baby,' she agreed. She twirled her martini on the rocks with her finger. She licked the finger thoughtfully. 'All you really know is that a lot of people have been knocked around, Jo-Jo Olsen has vanished, and someone is looking for him besides you.'

'Thanks,' I said. 'I know a lot.'

She was right, of course. That was all I really knew. I had a lot of guesses and a lot of possible connections, but what she had summed up was all that I really knew. Except that my client was in hospital and that for fifty bucks I had a good chance of joining him and that I could not get out of it now with any self-respect. Not with my client almost beaten to death. I could not even get out of it without self-respect. I thought of nicer things.

Marty was wearing a slim grey jersey skirt that curved well and had those folds across the belly that a woman with hips but no belly always has in her skirt. She wore a black turtleneck silk jersey top without jewellery and a grey jersey jacket like the coat of a man's suit but tailored for a woman. On the jacket she wore a silver, star-shaped abstract pin I had given her. Her long suede coat was over the chair. Most of her clothes are tailored and stylish.

When she had first come to New York to be an actress she had dressed casually; she really cared little for clothes. But casual clothes got more stares these days, and she lived all night with stares since taking the job in the girl-show at Monte's Kat Klub. (She had had to face the truth that it was not going to be easy to become an actress.) Most of her clothes covered her from knee to throat for the same reason. She favoured high turtle-necks. She said that she could not stand to be exposed even an inch below her throat when she came off the stage, where her working clothes might have had trouble covering a three-year-old midget.

'You can't forget it? Walk away?' she said.

'No,' I said.

'The boy?'

'Partly,' I said. 'I can't leave a client who's got more bandages than hair. It isn't done.'

'Do you think Jo-Jo killed this Driscoll girl?'

'No, but Gazzo does,' I said. 'No, Gazzo doesn't think that either. Gazzo doesn't think, he learns. He's a good cop. He'll find Jo-Jo before he thinks about guilt.'

'If anyone finds Jo-Jo,' Marty said.

'They're still looking,' I said. I drank my beer. 'What I don't figure is Stettin. How does he fit in? They took it all, but what did they want? The gun? The billy? The wallet? What?'

'Maybe just time,' Marty said. 'Maybe whoever did it is just cautious and wanted Stettin out of the way for a time.'

'She's young, Marty, but she thinks. She is too young for me, really, and I often ask myself why. I mean, why do I want a woman so young? All right, there is a normal reason—she's nubile as hell. But there is more. We worship the young in this country, and a lot of the world has begun to follow us. But what we worship isn't really the young, or even being young. It's *youth*— the hope and innocence and immortality of youth. We want to be young not because it is physically good to be young and virile, but because to be young is to not yet know that the world is transient, incomplete, and not often what we want it to be. You cease to be young that first instant when you know that nothing is complete and that nothing can last forever ' not even your own dreams and desires. To be young is to see the world through eyes that think that all is possible. And one way to feel young is to have a woman twenty years younger, more or less. Marty is my illusion of youth, and she's a smart girl.

'All right, someone wanted Stettin out of the way,' I said. 'For what? Just to knock over one apartment? To make a getaway? In the first place the burglary took place before the mugging. The getaway theory is out, Stettin saw nothing. He doesn't know why he was hit.'

'Baby, it could all be coincidence,' Marty said. 'All coincidence, or part coincidence. Maybe Stettin is the piece that doesn't fit. The patrolman isn't involved. Your Jo-Jo just saw the burglar and can place him on the scene of Tani's murder. Or maybe all Jo-Jo saw was who mugged the policeman, and the murder isn't part of it. Either murder.' She chewed her fingernail. 'What I don't understand, Dan, is something else. Those two men who are following you. I mean, are they Pappas' men, and if they are, why does he warn you and have you chased? They're not just tailing you, honey, they're after you, and Pappas could talk to you any time.'

I let her analyse. 'So?'

'So,' she said, 'who are the two men? Who would send men out against Pappas? I mean, if they aren't Pappas' men and they are after this Jo-Jo, then they must be out to cover up for the killer of Tani, and that means they are against Pappas. Who works against Pappas?'

As I said, Marty could think. Who, in our local underworld, worked against Andy Pappas? It was one of my very best unanswered questions.

'Maybe Olsen hired them without Andy knowing it just to make sure I laid off,' I said. 'Maybe they don't know they're bucking Pappas.'

Marty sighed, finished her martini. 'Maybe, maybe, and maybe. Honey, you know less than the CIA knew about Cuba before the Bay of Pigs. Maybe you're in the wrong business. They solve a case a lot faster on television.'

'In one hour flat, less time for the commercials,' I said. 'They're smart, and the criminals are co-operative. I've got no sponsor buying prime time. Maybe I'll never solve it.'

'If you don't solve it, baby, you won't be fit for human company. I know you. Your pride'll be hurt.'

'Right now I'd settle for hurt pride. They won't let me.'

'Think well then. I've got to go take my clothes off.'

She put on her suede coat, kissed me, and left. I sat on the bed and watched her go. Then I got up and went to the window. I opened the edge of the shades a crack. My eyes scanned the night street. I saw nothing but the usual crowd of a Friday night. There were no shadows lurking in the doorways. I watched Marty come out of the building below and cross the street.

She strode out like a racehorse, her suede coat open and swinging in the hot night. People, men and boys, looked at her, but she looked at no one. (In case you are wondering about that suede coat on a hot summer night, it's not a mistake. The Kat Klub isn't far from Marty's place, the girls often run out for a quiet drink, coffee, or hamburger between shows—who can afford Monte's prices—and like to be covered. Besides, there is always the off-chance of a raid, and the girls have a coat all the time just in case they have to ride the wagon.) I watched her turn the corner and disappear. I felt a sudden sense of loss. I always do. That is what love means; that you feel a loss every time you see her vanish from your sight.

I went back to the bed but I felt restless. The truth was that I was tired, but that I knew I should be working on something. Or perhaps the real truth was that I was comfortable here, I felt safe here, and I did not want to leave to go out where there was danger and uncertainty. I had that inertia that comes when you can't think of anything to do that you feel optimistic about. I did not care if I never heard of Jo-Jo Olsen again. I could think of nothing that would be worth doing, that gave me a reason to think that I would learn anything important. Which was also not true.

I had not really talked it out with old Schmidt before Petey was beaten and I went to the hospital. Schmidt had been on Water Street all the day last Thursday, he might have seen something he didn't even remember. Then there was Petey. He should be able to talk a little by now. I could ask better questions now, especially about the Driscoll girl.

There was the Driscoll girl's building. Someone might have heard something that would mean more to me than to the police. And there were her other men. There was a great deal I could do. Too much. There is a kind of paralysis that comes when there seems to be too much to get done.

I got up and went out into the kitchen for another beer. Then I turned on the television and sat in Marty's best easy chair. I told myself that I would think while I watched TV. By the end of the latest super-spy show I had still not begun to think. I liked the TV show. It was so intricately simple, so complex and yet childish. All fuss and feathers around the most simple of concepts—the chase; the Keystone Kops. A beautiful comic-book world where the utterly impossible has such a real surface and where every possible terror is looked at, but there are no surprises.

After the show ended I had no chance to think.

I had left my chair to look again out the window. The street was clear. Nothing but Friday night revellers beginning to build up steam as midnight approached and the shank of the night was at hand. Then I heard the noise in the hallway outside the door.

Footsteps walked lightly in the corridor, but with no attempt to be silent. Two men from the sound of the steps. Then they stopped—outside the door of Marty's apartment. I saw the shadows of their feet beneath the door from where I stood silent in the dim apartment. The blue-white light of the TV was behind me. I looked around for a weapon.

The doorbell buzzed.

I stood there and looked at the door. The doorbell buzzed again, nice and polite but a little more insistently. Somehow I did not think the two unknown men who had been watching me would have rung the doorbell. But I waited for the third ring, prolonged this time, and then the voice.

'Open it up, Fortune!'

A voice I knew, but for a moment I did not place it. It was a familiar voice, but not that familiar.

'Come on, buddy boy, we know you're in there.'

I got it. Jake Roth. It was the voice of Andy Pappas' best gun. I went to the door and opened it. Even if I had been worried about Roth, I would have opened the door. Roth would have kicked it in within seconds anyway. I saw that the tall, skinny killer was not alone. He had Max Bagnio with him, a little apart and a step or two behind to Roth's right with a clear view of the door. Little Max had his hands in his suit coat pockets. Roth eyed me up and down with those snake eyes. His long neck angled forward as he made a quick survey of the room behind me.

'Tell us we can come in, buddy boy,' Roth said.

I stepped back. 'Sure, come ahead.'

Roth and Max Bagnio ambled into the room like the well-trained team they were. They duplicated no effort. Each surveyed a section of the room. Roth checked what had been out of sight from the doorway and checked the kitchen. Bagnio took the dark corners, the bedroom, and the bathroom. They shared the closets. They came together again in the living-room where I stood. They had been in position to cover each other the entire time, and they had not spoken a word.

'Andy send you?' I asked.

They were still looking around from where they stood in the living-room. They had not actually looked at me since coming into the apartment. Max Bagnio seemed disappointed. I felt cold. Bagnio was looking for Marty. Little Max was disappointed that Marty was not there. I'm not even a woman and I shuddered at the thought of his hands on me. (Maybe if I had been a woman I would not have shuddered. Women have their own values.) Roth wandered around looking under pillows and cushions.

'*Mister* Pappas sent us, peeper,' Roth said.

None of Andy Pappas' men can understand why Andy lets me talk to him the way I do any more than I understand it myself. They have seen men have both arms broken for much less. This does not seem to bother Bagnio much, he is only curious. What Andy does is gospel to him, but he is interested. Roth was bothered. Roth did not like me calling his boss Andy. It seemed to annoy him.

'What can I do for Andy this time?' I asked, rubbing the first name in.

Roth still had not looked at me again. The vulture-like gunman dropped a chair cushion as if disappointed that he had not found at least an old garter. He turned to me. He hit me flush on the mouth. I never even saw the punch coming. All I saw was Roth, a thin smile of very good capped teeth, and then I was sitting on the floor.

'You're still asking questions,' Roth said.

I shook my head to clear it. Roth hit hard for a skinny man. I guessed that he was all muscle, like a whip. I tasted blood. My lip had already begun to swell. A tooth felt loose. I shook my head again and got up. I got halfway up. My hand was still on the floor. Roth hit me again. He hit twice. The right caught me on the cheek, I think, and the left hit my nose. The right lifted me up, and my nose was directly in the line of the left. I remember thinking that Jake Roth had not done it properly. He had led with his right. Very poor boxing.

'You talked to the cops,' someone said. I think it was still Roth.

I saw Max Bagnio. He seemed to be standing over me. That was odd, because he had been behind me. I wondered when he had moved. Bagnio looked bored. The little gunman was still looking around wistfully for Marty, I think. Then I realized that Max had not moved, I had. The last two punches had knocked me across the floor beyond Bagnio. I was lying flat with my head almost under a chair. I could taste a lot of blood and my nose was numb. I guessed that it was broken. My cheekbone felt red hot. There were tears in my eyes. My head seemed to belong to someone else. My legs would not move. Then Max Bagnio seemed to float away. I shook my head and Bagnio came back. So did Jake Roth.

'You were told,' Roth said. 'We told you.'

His voice seemed distant, in some other room, although his face was close. The tone of his voice was one of hurt bewilderment. I had been told. By Pappas. By Jake Roth. And yet I had asked questions. I had gone to the police. Roth did not understand that. I had been told. It was confusing to Roth. His face bent close down over me. I felt his hands pinching my ears. He helped me up to a sitting position. The pinching was clearing my head a little. Roth leaned me against a chair. His face bent close.

'You didn't listen, buddy boy,' Roth said.

His hand slapped my face lightly. On the broken nose. It hurt.

'You got to listen,' Roth said.

His hand slapped again. There was a lot of pain. I felt the chair behind my shoulders. I leaned my left shoulder hard against the chair, pressed my left shoulder against the chair, and swung my right fist with all the strength I had. It hit Roth flush on the chin. I felt the punch go all through my arm and up to my nose. It felt good. It cleared my head for a moment. I saw Roth go over backwards and sprawl all long legs kicking in the air. He had been crouched and off balance and my punch had not been bad. I even saw a little blood on his face as he came back up. He came back up fast. He had been hit before, and I'm no fighter. But there was blood on his mouth. I guessed that he had bitten his lip when I hit. I grinned. He kicked me in the stomach.

'You dirty little son-of-a-bitch!' Roth snarled.

He kicked me in the side where I lay doubled up. His shoes were big and pointed. I felt hands picking me up. It was Max Bagnio. He sat me against a chair again. Max seemed to be holding Roth away now. I sat there and saw them argue. Then Roth leaned down again.

'You got it, buddy boy? You got it now?'

I hit him again. My strength was pretty near gone, the punch did not even knock him down. But it must have made him crazy mad. He did not hit me, and he did not kick me. Maybe he had decided, somewhere in that vicious and cunning but not too intelligent brain, that kicks and punches were not doing the job. I felt his hands on my throat. I was lifted. And then I seemed to hurl through the air and hit a wall with a crash.

I was on a floor, and it was cold. Somehow my brain was still working. I felt a little like the time I had been torpedoed and had had a concussion but somehow had been able to think clearly enough to get over the side and into the raft and even help row the raft. I knew that I was not functioning, not well, but perhaps enough. Anyway, I felt the coldness of the floor and realized that Roth had thrown me into the kitchen. By the neck like a chicken.

I think it was that thought that made me mad—like a goddamned chicken.

I shook my head and looked around. Roth was coming towards the kitchen. It all seemed to be in slow motion, distant. I got to my knees and counted the drawers in the kitchen cabinet. I opened the one I wanted. I took out the heavy, fifteen-inch butcher knife. It had a razor-sharp edge. I had sharpened it for Marty myself. I fell back down with my back against the cabinet, sitting up, the butcher knife in my hand. I made a hell of an effort, and the room came clear. Roth and Bagnio were both in the kitchen doorway.

They had their automatics in their hands. I suppose that was actually a reflex action for them as soon as they saw the butcher knife. They both stepped into the kitchen. They stood apart so that I could only get to one of them at a time. The kitchen was small with little room to manoeuvre, and I was sort of wedged into a corner against the cabinets. I looked straight into the muzzles of those two guns. Roth laughed.

'A stinking shiv against two guns! You'd die real quick, sucker. I'll gun you before you move a hair.'

'Put it down, Fortune,' Bagnio said.

'No closer,' I said. My voice sounded strange even to me. My lips were swollen like balloons. My jaw hurt. My nose had begun to throb like a hammer.

Roth was pale. 'I'll kill you, buddy.'

'You'll have to,' I said. I held the knife.

Bagnio took a step. 'Listen, Fortune . . .'

I flicked the knife in front of me. 'You'll have to kill me. Get close again and I'll kill you. You want me, you better use those guns. Come near me and I'll kill you.'

I meant it then. I had been hit hard enough and often enough to mean it. I really meant what I said. I had had enough.

But I was also thinking. Roth and Bagnio had no orders from Andy to kill me; I was sure of that. I counted on that. I hoped I was right. Not that it mattered. If they had orders to kill me, they would do it one way or the other. There was a chance that if they shot, I might be able to knife one of them. No, there was no chance. The automatics were both .45 calibre. Roth pointed his.

'Jake,' Bagnio said.

'Beat it if you don't like it,' Roth said.

'Let's go, Jake,' Bagnio said.

I heard his voice. Bagnio was uneasy. I was sure of it. Bagnio was nervous. Something was bothering Little Max more than a beating should have bothered him. Especially a beating ordered by Andy Pappas. Maybe I was wrong.

'This dirty bastard punk,' Roth said.

'We done the job,' Bagnio said. 'He got the message.'

I'm not even sure when they left. I found myself alone on the kitchen floor. I thought I remembered Max Bagnio looking back in the kitchen doorway, saying, 'Take it easy, Fortune.' A testimonial. Max Bagnio was giving me a salute, man to man. The way the Zulu warriors had saluted the surviving British soldiers at Roark's Drift after about one hundred British had held off eight thousand or more Zulus for a whole day and night and the Zulus had given up. Bully. That was why the Zulus had lost in the end.

I remember the pain building.

I remember thinking that not only my nose was broken when the pain grew in my side and chest.

I remember Marty's face bending over me.

I think I remember the doctor.

I know I remember the pain.

CHAPTER 13

The first time I woke up I concentrated on where I was. That is an old reflex of a drifter like me. I was in a bed. There was sun outside drawn shades. The furniture was not my own bedroom. It did not look like the room in the Hotel Manning. It was not jail, and it was not a hospital. It was a problem, but I gave it up. I was more interested in the pain.

The second time I woke up I concentrated on how I was. My head was light and not attached to my neck. There was a headache in the head that floated somewhere above the bed. My face was swollen. There was a bandage of some kind on my nose. I ached all over. I seemed to be strapped across the ribs. But I also seemed to be all there.

I thought about what had happened. I knew I had been beaten by Jake Roth, but the details were confused. The thought of Roth must have been on my face.

'You look like you're seeing a ghost.'

It was Marty. I was, of course, in her bedroom. She stood with a tray. I saw orange juice, coffee, a bowl of something that steamed. I was hungry.

'I am,' I said. 'Mine.'

She put the tray down on the bed table and gave me the juice.

'You found me last night?' I said.

She nodded. 'In the kitchen. You had a butcher knife. Did you . . .?'

'All take and no give,' I said.

Then I recalled my two punches. That pleased the hell out of me. At least Roth would have a sore mouth today. I also remembered my ultimatum. That made me feel cold. It is one thing to take a chance like that in the heat of action and another to think about it later. Jake Roth wasn't a man filled with logic or self-control. He could have lost his head.

'When I saw you I nearly fainted. I saw the knife, you looked dead. When I found you were just out cold, I called the doctor. He said it looked worse than it was.'

'It feels worse than it looks,' I-said. 'What's the score?'

'Broken nose; you won't be so handsome.'

'That could help.'

'Facial bruises, a lot of them. Cuts inside and outside on your face. A mild concussion and a cracked rib. Some torn ligaments in your chest, too. I'm so sorry, baby.'

'I bet I look grand,' I said. I smiled. It hurt.

'You'll need a visit to the dentist, too. Who did it, Dan?'

'Just forget it,' I said. 'You should have shipped me home.'

'Yes I should have!' Marty said. 'Now eat. Soup is good.'

I had the soup. It was good.

'What did they want?' Marty said.

'No questions,' I said. 'I was stupid to come here.'

'Finish your soup.'

I finished the soup and the coffee. She sat on the edge of the bed and watched me until I had finished. Then she leaned and kissed my forehead. She stood up.

'You stay here.' she said. 'And try to do something more constructive than being a human punch bag.'

'Where do you think you're going?' I said.

'Work, baby,' she said.

'Work?'

'It's almost nine o'clock.'

'At night?'

''The doctor gave you a shot. He said you need at least two days in bed—alone.'

'I slept all day?'

'You did, and you looked cherubic,' Marty said.

'Sure,' I said.

'Two days the doctor said.'

'Sure,' I said. 'You go to work.'

'You'll be here when I get back, Dan?'

'Maybe,' I said. 'No, baby, I doubt it.'

'Meaning you might come back, but first you'll go.'

''The best defence is a good offence,' I said.

She kissed me again. 'Be careful.'

Her hair shone red in the soft light of the bedroom as she left. She was wearing a turtleneck black sheath tonight, and carrying the suede coat. I wished she did not have to go. I wished that I did not have to go. But she had to work and so did I.

It looked like Pappas was a hell of a lot more involved, and worried, than it had seemed. Andy had never had me worked over before. I must be getting awfully close to some sensitive toes. They figured to be Pappas' toes, and yet I still did not like the setup. If Andy wanted me out of the way, he would be more direct, I was sure. And I trust in Gazzo's judgment. Not all the way, I could not rule Pappas out of it all, but if Gazzo did not see Pappas or his boys as the killer of Tani Jones, he was probably right. So if Pappas was not the killer, he must be looking for the killer. Then why work me over? To get to Jo-Jo exclusive? Yes, that made sense— Pappas-sense. He wanted Jo-Jo all to himself. It had to be. And that meant Jo-Jo had real problems. If I was to do anything but run away from it I had to get moving.

I started by getting out of bed. I was sore everywhere. The tape on my ribs helped, but it was hard to breathe. It was harder to breathe through my broken nose. My clothes were gone. I began to swear at Marty, when I opened the closet and found a whole change of clothes. She must have called Joe. It was good to have friends. I dressed and then took my first look into the mirror.

The broken nose hardly showed, except for a thick piece of tape across the bridge. There was tape on my cheekbone, and on my jaw. I was bruised, cut, and swollen. My lips looked like a hamburger bun, my gums looked a little like the hamburger. But it was the eyes that were prettiest. They were both that sick shade of dark yellow-brown-black for over two inches all round. I looked awful.

Before I got out of there I looked out of each window to see if I had any shadows lurking. I saw none. I went down the stairs warily, and before I left the entrance I surveyed all the doorways I could see. The Saturday night crowds did not make it easy. An army could hide in the mob of beat kids, students, bagel babies, and drunks. I saw no suspicious characters. Just in case, I took a few fast twists down side streets and through alleys and back yards to see if I could flush anyone. I drew a blank. No one was following me. I straightened my course for Doyle Street.

My course was obvious—too damned obvious. I had to start around again. Whatever Jo-Jo was, he seemed to be a good rabbit. No one had found him yet; not even Pappas if Pappas was after him. One fact stood out like a bikini blonde at a Quaker meeting: Jo-Jo had not seen fit to tell his family where he was, or whoever was after Jo-Jo beside myself had a reason for not asking the family. I put my money on the former—Jo-Jo had not told his family, which gave me a lot to think about. Why had Jo-Jo not told his family? It was a new question. Maybe old Schmidt would have an answer. Or Pete. After Schmidt, Pete would be my next stop. After Pete I would finally have to start the long round of travel depots. I did not look forward to that.

The murder block of Doyle Street was on top of the river. It was dark and deserted even on a Saturday night early. The West Side Highway stood raised at the far end, with the shadows of piers beyond it, and then the river. The apartment house where Tani Jones had died stood like a giant among shabby pygmies on the north side of the street near the east corner. An alley ran beside it, as Gazzo had said. I entered the alley beside the new building and walked through to Water Street. Schmidt's Garage was just down from the Water Street end of the alley, on the north side of the street. The alley where Stettin had been mugged was far down on the south side of Water Street near the river. I crossed Water Street and stood where I could see the alley beside the building, Schmidt's Garage, and the far-off mouth of the alley where Stettin had been attacked.

I could see the rear entrance to the building where Tani Jones had died. It was in the alley with a light over it. There was a ramp down to the garage of the building. The building itself towered above all the buildings on Water Street. Most of its windows above the seventh or eight floor were visible from Schmidt's Garage. It had no fire escape. There was little cover in the alley beside the building. I walked on down to Schmidt's Garage.

The entrances to both alleys were in plain sight from in front of Schmidt's Garage, but nothing more could be seen; nothing inside either alley. But someone driving up and down the street on a motorcycle could have seen almost anything in either alley. I did not search the alleys. The police would have combed them both, people walked through them all day, and cars and trucks used them by the dozen.

I looked around to be sure I was alone. Cars were parked on both sides of the street, bumper to bumper at this hour, except in front of the alleys and the two driveways of Schmidt's Garage. They were even parked in front of the two loading docks of a warehouse next to Schmidt's now that it was night. I looked at the garage and saw there was light inside the office as well as in the garage itself. At least Schmidt worked late and would have time to talk to me. It was a good omen.

Then I heard the bad omen. Silence.

A garage is not a quiet place. With light in both shop and office there should have been noise. There was no sound of any kind. I looked into the office. It was empty. There was an open ledger and a paper coffee cup. I went into the shop section.

I found Schmidt in the rear behind a stripped-down truck. They had worked him over good before he died. I did not think they had intended to kill him. He had just died on their hands. His white hair lay in a pool of blood that had poured from his nose and mouth. The blood was still wet. His bloody face was a mass of bruised wounds. It looked like at least one arm had been broken. I did not look for the rest of the details of what they had done to him, but a blow-torch burned on the workbench. There was a long steel rod in his right hand. It looked like he had fought back at some point. Some old man.

Fight had not helped. He was dead.

I went into the office and called Gazzo. I smoked while I waited. I had the feeling that eyes were watching me. That was probably only nerves, but the blood was still wet out there in the garage, so I was wary. A man came in to ask if I had a cigarette machine. I told him no, but I tried to keep him there. He had a girl out in a car and he left. I smoked and listened to every sound until the sirens growled into the street and I was surrounded by blue uniforms. Gazzo sat at Schmidt's desk. I told him my story of this killing.

'You better take a vacation,' the captain said. 'I can't handle many more bodies.'

'Bodies are your business,' I said. 'You live on dead bodies, Captain.'

I suppose I felt bad. And nervous. Schmidt had been a good, tough, honest man. None of it had helped him.

'I don't want the next to be yours,' Gazzo said.

He had seen my face. I did not want the next to be me either.

'You're getting close,' Gazzo said. 'Schmidt is still warm. You're maybe too close. You've maybe got someone worried. You want to tell me why?'

'I don't know why,' I said. 'I don't know anything.'

'Sure,' Gazzo said. 'Someone worked you over for fun.'

'They think I know, Captain, but I don't.'

He looked at me. 'That's bad.'

'I know how bad it is,' I said. And I did. It is bad enough to know something dangerous enough to be beaten for; it is much worse to not know what they think you know.

I went out into the dark of Water Street. Squad cars blocked the street. Their red revolving lights played across all the parked cars. I thought about Schmidt. The killers were still looking for answers. I did not think they had found any here. I took deep breaths in the hot night. I almost wished they had found their answers, ended it all. I lighted another cigarette. At a time like this the dangers of cigarettes don't seem so bad. You have to live a while for them to kill you, and I'm not sure many of us are going to make it. The men who control the bombs wear better clothes and speak better in more languages than Pappas or Jake Roth or the ones who killed Schmidt, but they are the same men.

I smoked and watched a solitary patrolman walk along the dark street. He was not one of the squad-car boys; he was a beat cop. Stettin's replacement. I watched him and smiled. He had come round the corner, and caught my eye, at a slow amble. He had probably been snoozing somewhere or cadging a quick free drink and had not heard the squad cars arrive. In the instant he saw the squad cars he assumed a purposeful efficient air. He came down the block batting car tyres with his billy, trying to appear tall and alert. He peered closely at the cars parked near the driveways and fire hydrants. He stopped at the cars parked in front of the loading docks. That was legal at night and on Sundays. He seemed annoyed that no one had parked illegally. I watched his slow progress down the block towards the river. I saw him pass the mouth of the alley where Stettin had been mugged. He looked into that alley.

There was a click inside my head.

That's the closest word I can think of. A click. A sudden sensation of something being released, of clicking into place. Where there had been all jagged pieces there was a click and a sudden smooth surface.

I knew where Officer Stettin fitted into this. I knew why he had been mugged. Suddenly, like that.

Not chapter and verse, not the full implications, but the connection. I was suddenly as sure as a man can ever be sure of anything. I did not know why I had not seen it before. It was so clear. So obvious. I knew what the mugger had wanted. I knew why Stettin had been attacked. The mugger had wanted the only thing taken from Stettin that could possibly have been a danger to anyone. The only thing taken that could have involved anyone else.

The summons book.

A guess? Yes. A hunch. But it had to be. Have you ever had a thought that you suddenly just know is true? Nothing else, you just know. That is sometimes all that detective work is—a flash of hunch that must be true. Sometimes, did I say? Most of the time. Ask any cop. All else aside, most of the crimes of the kind the police get—small, violent, messy crimes—are solved by informers or a hunch. Not clues, not a neat trail, but the experienced hunch.

I had the hunch I had been looking for. Stettin did not know why he had been mugged. There had to be a reason. And the only thing stolen that could have involved someone else was the summons book. End of hunch. Next question: How did a summons book become so dangerous?

Even as I thought I had begun to walk fast in the night. Towards St Vincent's Hospital. Because if my hunch were right, and I knew it was, then Pete Vitanza should be my confirmation even if he did not know it. If my hunch were right, then I had a whole new picture of the murder of Tani Jones. A picture I liked better. The picture I had sensed from the start. Burglars rarely kill, and Tani Jones had put up no fight. The shooting had been quick, close, sudden. The killer had not run. He was out looking for Jo-Jo. Looking hard to the point of two more murders. Why? Because there had been no burglar. There had been no robbery. That was all a cover-up.

Tani Jones had known her killer.

She had known her killer, and the killer had known her. He had known that she was Andy Pappas' girl friend.

The killer was a man who had called on Tani Jones. A man who went to see her while Pappas was safely out of town. A man who was cheating Andy Pappas with Tani Jones, the dumb little girl who liked men too much. Then what had happened in Tani Jones's apartment that day? I did not know that, a hunch can only go so far, but for some reason the man had killed her. When I knew who, I would probably know why, but one thing I was sure of—the man had not planned to kill Tani. The whole faked robbery had an impromptu ring about it, an aura of improvisation, a spur-of-the-moment desperate cover-up. Something had happened in Tani Jones's apartment that day that made a secret lover into a sudden killer.

What that was my hunch could not tell me, but my hunch told me one more big fact. After the killer had killed, faked his robbery, and got clean away unseen, something more had happened down on Water Street. Something had suddenly gone very wrong for the killer, and it had involved Patrolman Stettin and his summons book.

By this time I was at St Vincent's. The doctor did not want to let me talk to Pete Vitanza. I argued. I told the doctor that it was urgent police business. He had seen me there with Lieutenant Marx earlier. It finally worked. I went into Pete's room.

Pete was propped up in bed, his splinted arms thrust straight out. He looked better. He was young and resilient, and the young recover quickly. But his eyes were still bandaged, and when I entered his whole head turned towards the sound I made as I came in.

'Mr Fortune?'

He had had some visitors, there was mail on his bedtray and books on the bed he could not read yet. Apparently the nurse had been reading to him. But he was really waiting for me. Some of his visitors had been police, and he wanted to talk about Nancy Driscoll.

'It don't sound right, Mr Fortune,' Pete said. 'Jo-Jo ain't the type. The broad was chasin' him, you know?'

'Maybe he decided he wanted her after all,' I said. 'The police have a good-luck piece. Did Jo-Jo have one like it?'

'That little Ferrari?' Pete said. 'Hell.'

His hands rummaged among the opened letters on his bedtray. He came up with a key ring. On the ring, as he held it up, was another shiny red miniature Ferrari racing car.

'See?' Pete said.

'Jo-Jo had one just like it?' I asked.

'Sure, we got 'em together. I mean, here's another one, right?'

'You've got yours,' I said. 'Does Jo-Jo have his?'

'There got to be a thousand around the city,' Pete said.

'Fine,' I said. 'When we find Jo-Jo, and he has his, then the police will start looking for the other nine-hundred-and-ninety-eight.'

'He never killed her,' Pete said, but I heard the wavering in his voice. There was doubt in his voice.

'Who then?' I said. 'Maybe the two who worked on you?'

'It fits, don't it? I mean, she knew Jo-Jo, too.'

'Maybe,' I said, 'but now I want something else. I want to know everything that happened on Water Street a week ago Thursday. The day Stettin was hit. Everything, Pete.'

Petey shrugged again. 'We worked on the bike, drove around.'

'They killed Schmidt,' I said.

I saw the shudder go through him. Part of it was for Schmidt, I know that. Most of it was for himself. I know that, too. We think about ourselves. That's the way it is. Ourselves here and now, that's how we think. Most of the time most of us don't even care that the ship is sinking as long as we can make a good buck selling life preservers before it goes down and be rich for a little while. Ask any soldier who ever prayed that his buddy would be killed instead of him. That same soldier might toss himself on a grenade and save ten men and die doing it, but that is a different thing. That's not thinking about it. And that's not most of us.

In the bed Pete Vitanza was remembering the feel of their fists, the kick of their shoes. They could return.

'That's rough,' Pete said.

'Anything at all out of the normal,' I said.

Pete shook his bandaged head. 'We worked on the bike. We ate lunch at the bike. I mean, what's normal? Jo-Jo took the bike out. I took the bike out and around. We practised turns. Jo-Jo made these figures, you know, like figure-eights. He liked to stunt with the bike. So . . .'

'Stunts? Turns?' I said. 'You needed space maybe?'

I closed my eyes. I saw the parked cars on Water Street. The two driveways out of the garage and the loading docks. There were just two parking spaces between the driveway out of the garage and the first loading dock.

'You needed room for the manoeuvres?' I said.

I saw the reaction. Under the bandages he reacted.

'You moved a car?' I said.

'A black convertible,' Pete said. 'Yeh. We shoved this small, black convertible down by the loading dock. We laughed.'

One of those little things that happen and you never really remember. Like stopping to mail some letters on your way to work, and later you don't remember it and wonder why you were five minutes late for work. Or the time you find some debris on your lawn and you cross the street to drop it into a waste can. That puts you on the wrong side of the street. When someone says they saw you on that side of the street you tell them they must be wrong because you never walk on that side. Why would you cross the street?

'We needed some more room,' Pete said. 'This convertible was blocking the turns. It was unlocked. We just had to push it so Jo-Jo could make the stunts, yeh.'

'Then what?'

'Nothin'. We just shoved it down.'

'You said you were both at Schmidt's until six o'clock?'

Pete thought. 'No, I had to get home, you know? I guess I left first. Jo-Jo he hung around to finish up, cover the bike.'

'Did you talk to Jo-Jo again?'

'Sure, maybe a couple of hours later. And Friday, too. Early like. He said he was busy, couldn't work on the bike. I told you.'

'Did he say anything else? Maybe about that car?'

'No,' Petey said.

I stood up. 'Okay, you rest. The doc tells me the bandages come off maybe Monday.'

'You got to find him,' Pete said from behind his bandages. I mean, they already killed Schmidt and the Driscoll broad.'

'I'll find him,' I said. But in what order? First or second?

On the dark –street in front of St Vincent's my eyes took in everything that moved and all the shadows. I was jumpy. I felt like a spy on his first day in a strange city—all alone and not sure I could pass the first challenge. This was not my city now. It belonged to a killer. A killer who could hire men to look for Jo-Jo, and maybe for me. Two shadows who had no names and no faces, but who killed just for answers. It was their city now, because now I had some answers to give.

Patrolman Stettin had ticketed that black convertible because Jo-Jo and Pete had shoved it down into a no parking zone. It was all that made sense. The killer had come back to his car and found that it had been tagged. For some reason this was dangerous. Probably because it placed him on the block at that time, and for some reason that was very bad for him. Was it bad because it told the police, or told Pappas, or both? I did not know. But it had to be that he found the tag, hunted Stettin, mugged him, and took the summons book. That was one big answer. It left me with a big question: If the killer had the ticket and the summons book, why was he after Jo-Jo?

I was no longer in front of St Vincent's. All this time my feet had been walking. My feet were taking me where I had to go next, where I would get the rest of it. I was not sure I wanted the rest of it. When I pushed this time it would be too late to back off and think. One more push and I could not turn back.

CHAPTER 14

I stood at the head of the block where Swede Olsen and family lived in their gaudy sewer and watched all the shadows around me. This street was dark, but it was not deserted. In the hot summer night the stoops and fire escapes and sidewalks were festooned with men in vests and women in house-dresses. They had carried chairs and boxes out of their stifling rooms and sat in silent apathy. Some rested on the kerb. The women stared into nothing. The men drank from beer cans. From time to time someone moved, talked. It was, after all, Saturday night. The free time. The happy time.

I went down the block, and they barely looked at me. They did not care about me. They did not see me. They were too busy trying to see themselves. I passed them and climbed the few steps into the vestibule of the Olsens' building. The downstairs door was open on the hot night. I blended into the shadows of the dim downstairs hallway. I stood there for some time. There was no one suspicious on the street outside. Had they learned something from old Schmidt after all? If they had, it had probably been too late for Jo-Jo for some hours now. I was sure they had learned nothing from Schmidt, but where were they? I did not like the feel of it. I felt things closing in.

I climbed the stairs. Doors were open all through the tenement. The rooms inside the open doors were dark, because lights give off heat. Phantom shapes moved inside the dark rooms. The blue-white light of television sets flickered. Electric fans whirred. I went on up, slowly, and no one even turned a head to look at me.

The Olsens' door was closed. The Olsens had more on their mind than the heat. I pressed the button and waited. I knew, of course, that I was taking a risk. I had been warned to lay off. This visit to the Olsens would be the final push. There was a big risk, but that is what life is in the end—the risks you take. If you never take a risk you never live. You just exist the way a carrot exists. I did not feel brave, I just had to go on living.

Swede himself opened the door. 'You're crazy, Fortune.'

His sons sat in chairs behind the big Norwegian. They got up as Swede spoke. The mother, Magda, was in a green dress that made her wrinkled face a nauseating yellow. She seemed, for an instant, unable to believe that I was actually there again. I did not see the daughter. I pushed in past Swede. The two boys came to meet me with their clenched fists. I felt Swede big behind me.

Before they could gather their wits and swing into action I started to talk. I hit them with every hunch I had and every word I could remember. No names and a lot of guesses. It's an old police method.

'He came back and found that Stettin had tagged the car, right? After he killed Tani Jones he came back and found that Jo-Jo had moved the car; it was tagged, and he went out and got the summons book from Stettin. Then he came after Jo-Jo. Sure, I can see how scared you'd all be. I would be, with him after me. I'd be terrified. A man like that, big enough to try to buck even Pappas? Caught in the middle . . .'

No names, just 'he', and it sounds like you know more than you do. If the other man is confused, scared, he will usually slip. The other man knows, he has the secret inside his mind, and all at once under the barrage of words he assumes that you too know. It slips out. He tries to defend himself, and out it comes. I've used it a hundred times in divorce cases. A guy thinks his wife knows, and I make him think that; and out it comes.

'. . . There he was cheating on Pappas, making a big play for Andy's girl friend. Then, bang-bang, he kills her. Man, I mean, he's got trouble. But he can get away all right. Then he gets to the car—and it's been tagged. People know he's on the block. Jo-Jo knows he's on the block. He had to try to kill Jo-Jo! Jo-Jo saw him! What else could he do but try to get Jo-Jo?'

Swede Olsen shook his head at me. The two sons looked like death. I suppose it was death they were thinking about. Even Magda-the-rock blinked those washed-out eyes and seemed hypnotized as I talked. You see, they knew. Like the guilty husband or wife in a divorce mess, they knew and they thought I knew. They thought, I made them think, that I knew more than I did. But I did not have it quite right, you see? They were sure now that I knew too much, but I had it a little wrong. They had to explain to me where I was wrong, why it was not as bad as I made it seem. At least the weakest link did, and that was Swede. Swede and his big boys. Swede was up to his eyes in guilt, and that is the real trap. Swede had been living with it too long. He had to explain how I had it wrong.

'No, he don't hurt Jo-Jo,' Swede said, insisted. 'He won't never hurt Jo-Jo. Jo-Jo don't see nothing, and he ain't gonna say nothing, see? Okay, he got the lousy ticket, only he ain't gonna talk. Jake he knows it's okay.'

'Don't make me laugh,' I said. I laughed. 'A murder rap?'

'Jake he don't hurt Jo-Jo,' Swede insisted, tried to convince himself. I suppose he had convinced himself up until then.

'Dumb Jo-Jo got to grab that ticket,' one of the boys said.

'Stupid jerk,' the other boy said.

'Shut up!' Magda Olsen said, shouted, raged. 'Shut up!'

Magda had seen the trap. She had sensed the trick I was playing out. She tried to stop them. But Swede had lived with his doubt too long.

'Hell,' Swede sneered, 'it's okay. Jake he won't hurt Jo-Jo, but he'll take care of this creep. You're through, Fortune. Jake, he'll handle you good.'

Jake. There it was. At that moment, as I watched all of the Olsens, one thing only was going through my mind—a thought, almost out of left field: If Max Bagnio had not been in Marty's apartment last night, I would be a dead man now.

Jake Roth had not dared to kill me with Bagnio there. Because Pappas would have wanted to know why Jake had killed me, and the reason was that Jake Roth had killed Tani Jones! That was the one thing Jake never wanted Pappas to know. And that was what was behind the whole mess.

Jake Roth.

It happens like some great discovery in science. Once that first small break comes, then it all fits. It is suddenly all clear. All the pieces come together. Of course Jake Roth.

Isolated facts suddenly assume a pattern. A distorted picture comes into focus. Jake Roth. A cold-blooded killer, not too bright but cunning. A big enough man to hire other men to go against Andy Pappas. Stupid enough to cheat on Pappas and animal enough to kill a dumb girl if he became scared. An animal who lived by violence and the gun, and violence had been the key all along. Of course Jake Roth, and my mind began to put the rest of the pieces together.

'Jo-Jo took the ticket off the car,' I said. I saw it in my mind, the action on Water Street that Thursday evening. 'He pushed the car. It was tagged by Stettin. Jo-Jo was afraid the owner of the car had seen him on the block all day. He thought that maybe the owner would guess who had pushed the car and got it a ticket. He figured the owner would be mad. So he took the ticket and thought the owner would never know. Sure, a kid's trick, a little prank, a funny move. Very clever. Just take the ticket, and the owner would never even know he had been tagged. Only Jo-Jo made a mistake, didn't he? Some mistake.'

While I talked I thought about Jake Roth. It was all obvious now. The way Roth had worked me over. The way Bagnio had become nervous. Pappas had not sent them. Jake Roth had been on his own time last night. Roth had brought Max Bagnio to make it look like Pappas had sent them—if he had come alone I might have been suspicious right then. After all, Roth knew what he had done, and he did not know how much I knew. Now my brain gave me the small incident that had been out-of-normal— the way Roth had pushed me too hard that day at O. Henry's with the message to lay off the Olsens. Pappas had already made the point. Roth had been too eager.

'What mistake did Jo-Jo make?' I said.

Swede shrugged. 'No mistake. Jake he saw that cop tag the car. From the window of the dame's place.'

I pictured the scene on Water Street. Tani Jones's apartment must be in the rear of the building on Doyle Street—with a clear view of the north side of Water Street. Jake Roth, with a dead girl in the room, saw Stettin ticket his car that had been pushed into a no-parking zone! Roth must have left on the run or as fast as he could while faking the burglary, and when he got to his car—the ticket was gone.

'Jo-Jo don't even know the car!' one of the boys said.

Roth had just killed Tani Jones, and his car had been tagged—with the licence number a matter of record. All right, why was that so bad? Even if the police managed to learn about the ticket, it only placed Roth on the scene. They still had to place

Roth inside the apartment of Tani Jones to make a charge stick. But the answer to this was clear enough. It wasn't the police that scared Roth; it was Andy Pappas.

Roth had had no business on Water Street that day. To be there proved he had lied to Pappas, and Roth certainly knew Tani Jones. Andy Pappas could put two and two together as well as the next man. He could do it better—Andy lived his life wary and suspicious of everything. The lie, the presence of the car on Water Street, and the fact that Roth knew Tani, would have made Pappas at least suspicious. Once suspicious, Andy would have found out the rest—he had ways.

All right, but what had made Roth think that Pappas would learn about the ticket and the car—even from the summons book? How could Andy find out about the ticket if it were turned in by Stettin? There was only one way. I remembered what Gazzo had said about Roth's alibi—Jake had been at the Jersey shore all day. The captain had said that the police knew that Roth's car had never left Jersey—his car!

'The car wasn't Jake's, was it? It was one of Pappas' own cars,' I said. That was the only answer. The car had been registered to Pappas, and therefore the summons could get back to Andy someday. 'Jo-Jo took the ticket. Roth couldn't even pay it if he had wanted to. Not much, but enough problem for Jake. He had to get the summons book from Stettin and then try to find the ticket.'

I could imagine Jake Roth standing beside that car and thinking it all out with the dead Tani Jones only moments behind him. The ticket placed him in the wrong place at the wrong time. It was big odds against Pappas finding out, even if the ticket wasn't paid—but there was a chance, a possibility. And a chance was something Jake Roth did not take if he could be sure by a little mugging and murder.

'Jo-Jo didn't recognize the car,' I said. 'He came home with the ticket, and you saw it.'

Swede nodded. 'I know the licence number. I mean, I drives for Mr Pappas and Jake sometimes. That number, it hit me right in the face.'

'You'd heard about Patrolman Stettin,' I said. 'We all had by then. You figured something was very wrong.'

'The stupid kid laughed,' Swede said. 'He don't even know the car. He shows me the ticket and laughs. Jake Roth is worried, and Jo-Jo he laughs.'

'How did you figure it was Roth driving the car?' I said.

'I know Mr Pappas is in Washington. I know Jake is at the Jersey shore. I know the car is at the shore. I know Jake he likes that Jones pig. I mean, a couple of times when Jake was drunk he talked about the Jones girl. I tell him he's crazy to fool with Mr Pappas' girl, but Jake says he can handle her.'

'So you saw the ticket, you knew about Stettin, and you guessed that Roth had been driving the car. You figured Roth was worried Pappas would find out he was cheating with Tani Jones. You knew Water Street was behind her building.'

'Yeh,' Swede said. 'I figured something like that.'

I nodded slowly. They were all looking away from me. They were studying the walls or the floor, examining their hands.

'Why did he kill Tani, Swede?'

Magda Olsen answered for Swede. 'Jake don't kill no one.'

I watched her. Her face was a rock. Unbreakable and impassive.

'You know better,' I said.

'We don't know nothing,' Magda Olsen said.

'Yeh,' Swede said quickly. 'We don't know nothing. Jake he don't kill no one.'

As usual, Swede talked too much. He did not see the ridiculous contradiction of his words. None of them did. Or they did, but they did not care. They had given me the official communiqué. That was their story: they knew Roth had killed no one, and they also knew nothing. But what about Jo-Jo? He had run.

I felt uneasy. Something was odd. They knew nothing, that was their story. They were behind Jake Roth—and yet Jo-Jo had run. Why?

'You figured that Roth wanted that ticket, and Jo-Jo had it,' I said. 'How come Jo-Jo didn't give it to Jake?'

Swede seemed to find something very interesting on the floor. 'We don't know Jake needs it so bad.'

I considered Swede, and thought about the time sequence. Jo-Jo took the ticket. Swede recognized the licence number. Swede guessed that Roth had been driving the car. Swede had heard about Stettin. Okay. But at that point, Thursday night, they did not know about the murder of Tani Jones. Her body had not been found until early Friday morning when the maid arrived.

'You found out by Friday morning,' I said.

Alert, they would have known about Tani Jones almost as soon as the police. They were behind Roth. By all the facts and rules of the Olsens' lives the affair should have ended with Jo-Jo giving the ticket to Roth, the Olsens remaining silent, and a sigh of relief from Roth. *Omerta,* the code of silence.

Or in this case, because the dead woman had been the woman of Andy Pappas, they could have gone to Pappas. Not the cops, no, that was not done, that was *Omerta.* But why not Pappas? That ticket, the story, given to Pappas might have got all the Olsens a medal—especially Jo-Jo. But Jo-Jo had run instead.

'Jo-Jo ran,' I said. 'Jo-Jo didn't give that ticket to Roth, or to Pappas. Why?'

It was one of the boys who could not remain silent.

'He don't like Mr Roth!' the boy snarled. 'He's a big deal, yeh! Sure, Jo-Jo he's too good for us.'

'A big race driver he's gonna be,' the other boy said.

Magda Olsen was purple. 'Shut up! Shut up!'

Jo-Jo did not like Jake Roth. Jo-Jo did not recognize a car of Andy Pappas' when his father, Swede, worked for Pappas. You remember that I said that it isn't the facts, the events, the overt happenings that tell a story? No, not the simple facts and events. Something else, and I could smell the something else in that room. The something else was the character of Jo-Jo Olsen. The character I had sensed all along—the difference of Jo-Jo. The reason why it had not all ended as it should have was that Jo-Jo did not share his family's way of life.

More. Jo-Jo did not only not share their ways, he opposed their way of life. To the point of not helping Roth and also to the point of not helping Andy Pappas. Jo-Jo Olsen was not regular. I could see it all there in the faces of the Olsens. The boys with anger on their animal faces not for Roth but for Jo-Jo. Magda Olsen—hard, cold, like a rock.

Swede himself must have been thinking all that I was. The big man shook his head slowly back and forth.

'Crazy dumb kid,' Swede said. 'Always a stupid, dumb kid.'

A crazy dumb kid. I saw it—and Jake Roth had seen it. Jo-Jo was not regular. How could Roth feel safe with a man who was not regular? Roth was a man who had to be sure. He was facing the cops, and he was facing the anger of Andy Pappas. If I had been facing the revenge of Andy Pappas I would have wanted to be sure—very sure. I would want that ticket, and I would want the man who had it. I would have wanted it fast. Especially if it was in the hands of a boy who was not regular, who could not be trusted to follow the code.

Only . . . and the uneasiness came again. The sense of something very odd. Because I realized that Jake Roth could not have known on Thursday night who had the ticket. If he had known, he would have been at the Olsens' in five seconds flat. He could not have known, because Jo-Jo had not run until Friday morning! Jo-Jo had remained at home, with the ticket, all Thursday night and into Friday morning. Which left a lot of hours between Roth learning about the ticket and Jo-Jo's rabbit act. Hours I did not think Roth would have let pass in peace if he had known who had the original ticket. And hours in which Jo-Jo should have already been running, if he was going to run at all, instead of waiting until Friday morning—if Roth had known it was Jo-Jo who had the ticket.

Then it hit me—hard. Jo-Jo had not run until the murder of Tani Jones had been discovered. Jo-Jo had not run until the Olsens must have known just how bad the trouble was that Roth was in. That was all that had happened between Thursday night and Friday morning that changed the situation. That and the fact that, apparently, Roth had learned who had the ticket. But how . . .

'How did Jake learn that Jo-Jo had the ticket?' I said. 'He didn't see Jo-Jo take the ticket, or even push the car. If he had, he would have been after Jo-Jo Thursday night.'

They were silent. I looked from stone face to stone face. I felt that uneasiness again. I felt something lurking there in the room just under the surface. I looked at Magda Olsen. She would be the one to say it, if anyone did. She said it.

'His name it ain't Roth,' Magda Olsen said. 'It's Lindroth. He changed it. Jake Lindroth. He's Norwegian.'

Swede explained. 'Jake, he got me in with Mr Pappas.'

'Norwegian,' Magda Olsen said, 'He's Lars's cousin.'

'My cousin, see?' Swede said. 'I owes him.'

'Lars he works for Jake, not for Pappas,' Magda Olsen said.

'Jake, he got me in,' Swede said.

I heard it. I got it. And I got something else. If I was afraid of Jake Roth, I'd want to be sure, too. I mean, if I knew something about Jake Roth that could get Roth a quick trip to the morgue or the bottom of the river or a shallow grave in the Jersey marshes, I would want to be very sure that Roth knew I was safe and regular and very silent. Especially if I worked for Roth, or with Roth. Jake Roth would not feel good about a cousin, a protégé, who held out on him.

'Jake got plans for Lars,' Magda Olsen said.

In my spine I felt a monster in the gaudy room. A monster that stirred, assumed a shape. Like something that looms up out of a swamp on a dark night. The silence of the room had a stink like the breath of the monster. Swede Olsen and his boys were not looking at me. Only the old woman looked at me. She was a tough old bird. She did not flinch. Nothing in this world is simple, easy. Courage and honesty and strength are not qualities that always serve the good. Many killers are brave. Magda Olsen was not a woman who flinched from the truth.

'All this what we got,' Magda Olsen said, 'is by Jake Roth. We owe Jake. All this, and more we're gonna get.'

She waved her bony hand to indicate the whole grotesque apartment. They owed Jake Roth the big-fish home in the small-pond world where they lived. They lived on Jake Roth, and on the more they hoped he would get for them. The old woman waved her arm to show me what they owed Roth. She gave me her Gibraltar face. A rock of granite, the face of Magda Olsen.

After a moment I said the words. 'You told Roth. Friday morning, after you heard about the murder of Tani Jones, you told Roth that it was Jo-Jo who had the ticket.'

The monster was out. It slouched in that room like some leering black shape without human form.

Swede Olsen sweated. 'I got to tell Jake. I mean, when I finds out how bad it is, I got to tell him. He was gonna find out, you know? He don't stop till he finds out. If he finds out and I ain't told him, you know what happens? I mean, Jake he got to trust me.'

'Sure,' I said. 'Jake got to trust you. That's important.'

Swede wiped his face. 'Listen, Fortune, I owe Jake. I got to tell Jake so he knows it's okay. I got to tell him he's safe.'

'So you found out he killed Andy Pappas' girl friend, and you had to show how loyal you are,' I said. 'And Jo-Jo? You know Roth can't trust Jo-Jo. Cousin or no cousin. You knew that.'

Swede was eager. 'I make Jo-Jo beat it. I tell Jake he knows we won't talk and I'll make Jo-Jo get out of town. I mean, I got Jo-Jo safe out of town, and Jake trusts me. See? Jake he was real grateful. He says it's okay. He don't got to worry, and Jo-Jo he's safe out of town.'

Then they all began to talk. At me. They all talked at me, the words tumbling out as if a dam had burst.

'Then you got to come around!' Magda Olsen said. 'You got to ask questions.'

'You got to talk to the cops!' one boy said.

'You got to tell them go look for Jo-Jo!' the other boy said.

'You got to kick it all up!' Swede said.

'You!' Magda said. 'You got to worry Jake!'

I looked at all of them.

'You're not worried?' I said.

The silence after that was like thick cream. A room full of heavy yogurt. If I could stand high enough I could have walked on that silence.

'You really thought Roth would leave Jo-Jo alone?' I said. 'Jake Roth? You really thought Jake would let a man he didn't trust run around with enough on him to hang him? Even without the ticket, Jo-Jo knew! Jo-Jo could talk to Pappas! Any time in the next hundred years!'

'Mr Roth is family!' Magda Olsen said.

I laughed at her. In her face. 'A fifty-fifty chance at best. Roth would kill his mother if she knew too much and he didn't trust her to keep quiet.'

But the old woman was tough. 'Mr Roth he says it's okay, you hear? Mr Roth he trusts us. Then you come around. You and that stupid dirt pig Vitanza. You come looking, you ask questions, you go to the cops!'

She raved at me, and I listened; and maybe she was right after all. Maybe Roth would have trusted the Olsens to keep Jo-Jo quiet as long as Jo-Jo never came back to Chelsea. Maybe I had put the boy's neck in the noose. It can happen that way when you start stirring up the muddy water. Maybe Petey Vitanza had crucified his friend by trying to help him. I did not think so, I knew Roth too well for that, but it was possible. Anything is possible; even that Jake Roth might stop short of being absolutely sure. But I had asked the questions. The water had been stirred up.

'Then?' I said. 'After I came around? What then? I got Roth worried, okay, but you knew he was worried. You know he is worried. You know he's looking for Jo-Jo right now! You can go to the cops now. Or to Pappas. You think Jake just wants to talk to Jo-Jo now?'

'Sure, talk,' Swede Olsen said. The big Norwegian said it to the floor, to his feet in those ridiculous two-toned shoes. 'Jake wants to talk to Jo-Jo, make it sure, you know?'

I think my mouth hung open. I know I laughed. It was more a snort than a laugh.

Magda Olsen's voice was clear and steady. She stood in that room as rigid as steel, and her voice was as hard as steel.

'Jo-Jo takes care of himself,' Magda Olsen said. 'Lars is an old man. We live good. We got five kids. We got one in college, yeh. All our life Lars he works like a pig on the docks. I work, I sweat. Like animals we live. Now we live good. Mr Roth, he's a cousin, he gets Lars work with Mr Pappas. Good work, good money, the best. Mr Pappas he's good to us because Jake Roth asks him to be good. In one day for Mr Pappas, Lars he makes more money than two months on the docks. He is too old to go back to the docks. We got five kids. We only got one Jake Roth.'

What do you say? Go on, tell me. You feel sick, sure, but what do you say? Do you tell them that no human being risks his child to help a Jake Roth? Sure, that's true. It's real easy to say, especially if you wear a white collar and drive to work through safe streets. Do you say that Lars Olsen and his worn-out old woman should go back and work themselves to death, risk all they have and what life they have left, to save their boy? It sounds good, only I'm not so sure how true it is. How far is a father responsible for saving his son from his own mistakes? How much must a mother endure in this life for her child? It's easy to feel sick when no one is asking you to give up all that you have, all that you want, all that you need. Does it matter if the needs are rotten? Who says which need is good and which bad? And what about the other four kids? Do you sacrifice one boy to give the other four a better life—a life they at least think is better? Lars Olsen back on the docks at his age could do nothing for his kids. Magda Olsen was already an old woman long before her time. One for four. Are you so sure? I'm not.

'You can go to the police,' I said. 'Maybe Pappas would be grateful.'

Magda Olsen had made her decision. 'With what? We don't know where Jo-Jo is.'

'You don't know?' I said.

Swede Olsen watched his feet. 'I don't want I should know. Jo-Jo he's okay. Jake is okay. Jake is a good man. He don't hurt Jo-Jo.'

Swede was still trying to convince himself. Maybe he was trying to convince his other boys. He was saying that he was, after all, a good father and a big man. He was telling me, his sons, and himself that he really believed that Jo-Jo would be all right. The old woman, Magda, did not bother. She knew. She knew the truth and she faced it. Jo-Jo was on his own. Magda Olsen had more important things to think about, consider, and she did not hide from the truth. She had decided about her life and where her duty lay.

I left them.

I did not feel well. Magda Olsen was a woman who faced the facts, and she knew where her duty was and what it demanded. I knew that, too. All the way down those dark stairs past the opened doors where shadows moved in silence inside the stifling rooms my feet hardly seemed to touch the stairs. My legs felt stiff, my feet almost numb. Because I had done it. I had stood up and rocked the boat. It was all out in the open. I could not prove anything, but I had told the world what I knew. I had told Jake Roth what I knew. Because it did not take much imagination to know that Magda Olsen would be on the telephone. She was probably calling Roth right now.

All along that dark street my head felt light and my legs were still like stiff boards. I was a marked man now. Unless I could stop Roth, find Jo-Jo, and get some proof, I was a dead man.

And I did not even know where Jo-Jo could be.

CHAPTER 15

In the hotel room I lay on the bed in the dark. The bottle was on the table beside the bed. A shot glass was full beside it. I had poured it, but I had not drunk it. Whiskey was not what would help now. I lay there with my hand behind my back and tried to think of what I could do next.

I had made it back to the hotel without being followed, as far as I knew. I had been careful. Dark alleys and the shadows close to the buildings. I had walked as fast as my stiff legs would let me. The light was an enemy. Every street I crossed had been like a glaring stage with me naked across it. And all the way I had thought about the Olsens. On the hot slum streets where the victims of this world sat on chairs and drank beer and tried to find some air to breathe. The slum-streets that had shaped the Olsens and was the world they knew. Streets where, on nights like this, the people of the slums know for sure that they are the victims. They are the people the TV commercials do not speak to. They are the people who never appear in the American Dream, or any other dream. All their dreams are nightmares. There is no escape, and nothing will ever change. They were born in a stacked deck, they will die to the roll of loaded dice. And on nights like this, or when the snow winds blow in winter, they know for a moment who and what they are. They know that all their cunning schemes fool no one but themselves. All their long-planned deals are so many useless motions in a game someone else invented and made the rules for. They know that only self-deception gives them the illusion of life. They are Olsens without the strength of Magda or the luck of Swede.

And they know, on hot nights like this, that they are not of the very few with the luck or the strength or the strange and unexplained psychological quirk to escape. They are not special, and how should they be? How many of us escape what we were born to, who we are, what we have? How many in the bigger, richer, happier world are asked to be better than they were born? Or even different? Here, in the slums of the Olsens, they know that what the people above them get without effort they can have only if they are very strong, or very lucky, or very special. There are no more special people in the slums than in the suburbs, and just as few can move out of the slums into the suburbs as can move out of the suburbs on to the estates. So what do you tell the Olsens? That they must fall back because they have climbed to where they are by false means? That they must go down again because to stay even as far up as they have come now requires a method that sickens the fastidious who have never been down? Do you tell them that in a dirty world, some dirt is good and some dirt is bad? They know better. They know that they have only learned what their betters above them have taught them, not by word but by deed. They know that they did not create Jake Roth and Andy Pappas, they only have to live with them. They know that there is only one man in a thousand who can be different, who escapes where he was born.

That was when, on my back in the dark hotel room where I was even afraid to light a light now, I thought about Jo-Jo Olsen. Because it looked like Jo-Jo was one of the few. (I suppose I had somehow sensed this all along. I know I had sensed this. It was why I had kept going.) Jo-Jo was the one in a thousand. He could be different. He had been on his way out. Only now the slum, the world of all the victims, had reached up to pull him back. The world that he rejected had him by the ankle, if not the throat, and was dragging him down. He needed help if he was not to sink, quietly and unnoticed, out of sight into the slime of his birth. He needed help, because he was one of the special, the different. That Roth could not trust him, ever, proved in one way how different Jo-Jo was. Jo-Jo himself had proved it in another way.

A regular in Chelsea, or perhaps anywhere in this world, high or low, had two choices when he was in the position Jo-Jo found himself in the moment he had that parking ticket. He could keep quiet and be trusted, or he could stay and turn that ticket over to Andy Pappas. He could have risked his family and turned that ticket over to Pappas. He could have thought of himself. Andy Pappas could make life good for a man who did him a favour. Pappas could keep him safe. As safe as a man could ever be when he chose sides in a hard game. To be safe, maybe rich, all Jo-Jo had had to do was betray Jake Roth and his own family. In Chelsea I know how that decision would go most of the time. (I know how it would go in the rest of the world, too, and the decision would be the same.) But Jo-Jo had taken the hard way. He had run out on it all. He had run with no safety from Roth, no protection from Pappas, no help from the police, and no shelter from his family. He had refused to join any side. That is the real path of danger.

In the dark of the hotel room where I lay on the bed like some small animal afraid of the light, I laughed aloud. I laughed, but I did not feel amused. Jo-Jo had taken the way of real danger, and he might have made it. After a time, if Jo-Jo did not appear to finger him, Roth might have decided to give up. But Jo-Jo had a friend, and the friend had come to me, and I had brought in the police, and now Roth would not give up. Now Roth would be sure. He would have to kill Jo-Jo. He would have to kill me. Before either of us got to the police or to Pappas.

So I knew I had to get to the police. I had known that since I walked down those stairs from the Olsens' apartment. There was nothing else I could do. Instead, I lay on the bed in the dark with the untouched whiskey beside me. Because what could I tell the police? Roth would kill me before I got to the police, if he could, and yet what could I tell them? But I had to get to the police, because once I reached them I would be safe. I would be safe, and, the way it was, it was all I could do to help Jo-Jo.

A telephone call to Gazzo, and I would be safe once they got here. If Roth or his boys didn't find me before the police arrived, I was safe. Because once I had told my theory, Roth would have no more reason to kill me. All he would have would be a greater need to kill Jo-Jo. Because what I had was no more than a theory. The police would need much more. Even Andy Pappas would want some proof. For Andy it would not have to be much, but a little more than my hunch. Roth would deny it all. The Olsens would not back me. No one else alive knew anything. Except Jo-Jo.

Jo-Jo would be on the spot, because Roth would be on the spot. He would not care about me any more, but he would care a lot more about Jo-Jo than he did now. The police, and Pappas, would check out my story. They would look harder for Jo-Jo. Roth could not let them find him. A dead Jo-Jo would prove nothing. More than ever, Roth would have to kill Jo-Jo before he could tell anything to anyone. And yet it was all I could do now to help Jo-Jo. At least it would make Pappas look for Jo-Jo and make the police really look. There would be some chance that they would get to Jo-Jo before Roth or his killers. And I would be safe.

I had the telephone in my hand when I heard the scratching.

I looked around. The only weapon was the whiskey bottle. I picked it up by the neck.

The scratching came again. Someone was scratching lightly on my door. I got off the bed as quietly as possible. Maybe whoever it was would go away. I reached the door and stood there in the dark trying not to breathe. I saw a faint shadow in the line of light that came under the door from the corridor.

The scratching came again. Small scratching, feeble, like an insect or some small mouse. There was an urgency to it and a lot of nervousness. Whoever was out there was becoming more desperate. It occurred to me that gunmen do not scratch on doors. I didn't think they did.

I could be wrong.

If I was wrong and I opened the door or even moved to prove that I was in the room, then I was as good as dead. My bottle would not get two of them. Maybe it was only one? I listened again. I heard nothing but a kind of quick breathing.

I opened the door.

A girl stood there. For a moment I did not know her at all. I had no interest in any girls at this point. I looked up and down the dim and sleazy corridor of the Manning.

'Let me come in, Mr Fortune,'

She was nervous, and she was urgent. She pushed past me. She was shaking. A very scared girl. Then I recognized her. The Olsen daughter! I closed the door and locked it again. I put the whiskey bottle down on the bureau. The girl was looking at my face.

'I had a chat with Cousin Jake,' I said.

The girl sat down. 'When? Tonight? I mean . . .'

I have seen fear, and I have seen terror. I have seen panic, and trembling and fright and cowardice. The Olsen girl was in terror. She could not control her hands. She could not remember how she had been taught to sit. Her knees kept coming apart. She crossed her legs. And uncrossed them.

'No,' I said. 'Not tonight. How'd you find me?'

'I followed you.'

'No,' I said.

'To the street. You were hiding, but I'm small, I know the streets. I've lived around here all my life.'

'What do you mean, "to the street"?'

'I saw you turn on this street. I didn't see you after that. I took a chance on the hotels. This was the third. I asked the man downstairs what room.' She looked at me. 'You . . . you're easy to describe.' She was looking at my arm.

'The man told you?'

'I gave him ten dollars.'

I believed that. My life was worth about ten dollars to the night clerk. I liked to think that if it had been men who asked, the price might have been twenty-five. (If it had been men, the price would probably have been zero. The clerk would have been too scared.) And she was right. I was not easy to hide. Not with my arm and my present scarred face. If a girl could find me, I was long overdue on the telephone to Gazzo. Then, I had been watching for men tailing me. I might have overlooked a girl while seeing men. I hoped that was true.

'What's your name?' I asked.

'Anna,' she said.

'Okay, Anna, what did you want to find me for?'

The girl shivered. 'She was on the phone. Magda. My mother, I mean. I was in the bedroom and I heard and when you left she went on the phone, you know? I mean, she called him right off.'

'Jake Roth?'

She nodded. 'You was just gone out. My father, he didn't look so good. But Magda, my mother, she says . . . she says . . .' The girl, Anna, looked at me. '. . . she says Jo-Jo he got himself into it. She says we got to go through . . . we got to trust Mr Roth. We . . .'

Like I said, it was not exactly a surprise. I was now anxious to get rid of the girl and get on the telephone to Gazzo. I was more than anxious. It was past time to think about my own skin. I wouldn't help Jo-Jo dead. I had no intention of being dead even if it would help Jo-Jo.

'Did you hear what she told him? Roth, I mean?'

'She didn't talk to him,' Anna said. 'He wasn't there.'

I think I had the feeling a con gets in death row when the governor decides maybe the state doesn't need his life.

'She didn't talk to Roth?'

The girl shook her head. 'No. Not yet.'

'She didn't talk to anyone?'

'No. She said to have Mr. Roth call her.'

It was at least a reprieve. But not much. Roth and his hired boys had been after me already. Only they had not been after me as hard as they would be if they had talked to Magda Olsen. It gave me a good chance that I could call the captain and have him get to me in plenty of time. I wanted my story on the record where it would do Jake Roth no good to silence me.

'Thanks, Anna,' I said.

The girl did not move to leave. 'You . . . you said Mr Roth would kill Jo-Jo. You said Roth would never trust Jo-Jo?'

'No, Anna, he won't,' I said. 'You've got to make your father go to the police. Or at least to Mr Pappas.'

The girl shook her head. 'They won't. All they said. And they're scared.' She looked up at me again. 'I know where he is.'

Well, I sat down. I had spent the whole week looking for Jo-Jo Olsen. I had not found him. I had decided that I could not find him. I was not sure I wanted to find him now. I had my course of action all mapped out, and a good chance that I would make it home safe. All I had to do was call Gazzo, get picked up, stay in the lockup a few days until everyone knew my theory, and then just stay away from dark alleys so Roth could not get at me easily just to punish me for talking. I had it all planned.

'You know?'

She nodded. 'He wrote me. Just a note. He used a typewriter and sent it to where I work. He says he's okay. He says he . . . here.'

She handed it to me. An envelope and a single sheet of paper. I took them. The envelope was typed, and so was the note. There was nothing in it that said it was from Jo-Jo. Just a few words that said he was okay, the weather was good, he was working at some small job to eat, the work was lousy, but at least he was around the cars, and don't worry. There was no signature and no address. Only that bit about the cars said it was from Jo-Jo, and maybe some things only his sister would know. The envelope had no address on it. But it did have a postmark. It was from Spanish Beach, Florida. Spanish Beach had a speedway.

'Who else has seen this?' I said. I guess I was looking for an out.

'No one. I . . . I was scared.'

'You're sure? No one else saw this? Not your family?'

'No one, Mr Fortune,' Anna Olsen said.

'Okay,' I said. 'Now you get out of here. We don't want anyone to see us together. That clerk might even call someone. You go home, and you stay there. Don't let anyone see you leave the hotel.'

She blinked at me. 'Will you . . .?'

'I don't know. I've got to think.'

I watched at the door until she was gone down the stairs. Then I went back into the room. I locked the door behind me. I went and stood at the window of the dark room and looked out at my city. It was not my city now, not as long as I had to hide in it. Their city, and I did not like that. The telephone stood on the table beside the bed. All I had to do was call, and I would be safe. Spanish Beach was not a one-street village, especially in race season. For all I knew to go to the police was still the only real way I could help Jo-Jo. Maybe the police could get to him first. Who was I to think that I could do better than the police?

But maybe I could do better. I knew a lot about Jo-Jo by now. The Spanish Beach police knew nothing. I knew in what kind of place to look, what kind of man to look for, and who I was up against. Jo-Jo would be hiding, using a phony name, probably a disguise; and maybe I could move just a little faster.

There was sweat under my arms and down my back. One phone call and I would be safe. The moment I stepped out of the room without the police I became a target, and there could be a gun waiting around every corner. Out of this room, on the streets, I was a rabbit in the open. Maybe, with luck, I could do just a little more than the police. Maybe I could find him just a hair faster.

And risk a bullet in the back of the head all the way.

A telephone call and I was out of it.

And Jo-Jo maybe had one hair less chance of living another day.

I took down the whiskey in that untouched shot glass in one good gulp.

Who was I kidding? I was going to try to find Jo-Jo. In the long run my only real safety lay in putting an end to Jake Roth. When you came down to it, every little bit would help. I was going to call Gazzo, yes, and I was going to Spanish Beach. I had started, I had to finish. No, that was not it. Not that I had to finish a job, or that I personally wanted to end Jake Roth. Simply that if I did not go and Jo-Jo was found dead, I would never know if maybe I could have saved him.

I put on my suit coat and went to the door. My hand was sweating. But I opened the door. I went down the back stairs, out the back way, and across back yards and through alleys for two blocks before I risked hailing a cruising cab. I told the cabbie to take me to Newark Airport. At Newark I got a seat on the first jet out—a non-scheduled carrier I knew that had a flight going out at 6 a.m. for Miami that would get me a good connection to Spanish Beach. It was really a cargo line, but I knew the boys. At least it would be a safe flight.

I had a long wait, and the airport was as safe as anywhere. I used the telephone in the non-scheduled office to call Captain Gazzo. For once the captain was out of his office. I left an anonymous tip that Jo-Jo Olsen might be in Spanish Beach, Florida. That was all. The captain would figure it out, and until I was under police protection I was not about to spill my guts in the open and tip Jake Roth. Jake had ways of finding out what the police knew. (I don't think there has ever been a police force without someone who could be bought at a price, and I don't expect that there ever will be.)

I waited for the dawn in a dark corner of the non— scheduled hangar. I smoked and watched the men at work loading the freight. I felt pretty set up with myself. I was being brave as hell. An honest detective and a good citizen.

CHAPTER 16

Spanish Beach was hot. A loud town, crowded now because the cars were racing. My connection had been good at Miami, and we came into Spanish Beach on time. I took a taxi straight to the speedway.

I remember when Spanish Beach was a sleepy town where they spoke more Portuguese than English and everyone fished for sponges from boats with eyes painted on their bows. Now it was too big and loud and fast. It was all speedway and fast cars, like Riverside, California, and Daytona Beach.

At the speedway the cars were practising out on the brick track, and the administration offices were open. From the letter Anna had received I was sure Jo-Jo was around the track in some small job. He was smart enough to stay away from the cars themselves. At least I hoped he was.

I found the personnel office and went inside. A man bent over papers behind a counter. There were tables. The busy man did not look up when he heard me.

'Nothing but selling programmes,' the man said. 'If that suits you, take a form and fill it out all the way.'

He was a small man with greying hair and a bald spot he carefully covered by brushing the hair sideways on—top of his skull. Ink stained his hands. He wore no coat, and his shirt was plastered to his back already.

'I'm looking for a man,' I said.

He looked up at that. He did not move, he just looked.

'A young guy,' I said. 'Blond, tall, about nineteen.'

He put down his pen. 'Who the hell are you?'

I showed him my credentials. He stood up then and came to look at them. He was only mildly impressed. He sniffed. He looked at my missing arm and at my face.

'I lost it on Iwo Jima,' I told him. 'Knocked out three Jap machine-gun nests. I'm a real detective.'

'Private,' he said. 'I don't have to tell you anything. Private cop and New York at that. Three Jap nests? All alone?'

'I had help,' I said. 'How about my friend? You probably took him on for some job last Saturday or Monday.'

'All I took on all week was programme kids.'

'Nothing else?'

'That's it.'

'You want to save the life of a programme boy?'

He laughed. 'Them? Between you and me, mister, they ain't worth saving. Punks, all of them. They take the job so they can watch the races. Race bums. Half the time they look at the races 'n don't sell a programme. The customers got to beg.'

The man was small and red and he had a pet peeve. So many people have a pet peeve. Something or someone or some group they have to hate. It gives them something to do in the world. It gives a shape to their lives.

'Talk to me and I'll take one off your hands,' I said. 'The name is Olsen, but he's probably not using his right name. Tall, blond, not bad-looking. No marks. He likes motors. You would probably have hired him around last Monday, like I said.'

The man shrugged. 'You just described maybe half of them. They come, they go. If they work a week they're veterans. You got a picture?'

I produced the picture Pete had given me. It hadn't improved any as a likeness of Jo-Jo. Besides, he would have done something to change his appearance a little. The man confirmed my opinion.

'Some picture,' the man said. 'It looks like most of them.' And the man looked hard at me. 'What's so important about this Olsen anyway?'

My stomach went down on an elevator about a hundred feet.

'Someone else was here?' I said.

'It's my day,' he said.

'When? How many of them? What did they look like? What did you tell them?'

'You got a lot of questions, mister.'

I laid a twenty on the counter. It hurt. The small man scooped it up. My war record and the twenty made him my friend.

'There were two of them. They left maybe an hour ago, no more than that,' and he went on to give me a pretty fair description of my two shadows. The same two who had certainly beaten Petey and probably killed Schmidt.

'What did you tell them?'

'What I'm telling you. I got no Olsen. The description fits about ten of the punks. Your picture don't change much. I can give you a list. The rest is up to you.'

'Did you give them a list?'

'Sure, they paid too,' he said, and then he seemed to stop and think. 'For the war record I'll do you a favour. I figure you ain't so far back of them.'

'How so?' I said.

'Well, I heard one of them telling the other that they should have come to the speedway first instead of wasting time asking people all over town and out in Flamingo.'

'Flamingo?'

'It's a small town just outside city limits. They got a dirt motorcycle track gives us some competition.'

'How do you figure that gives me some time?' I asked.

'Hold your horses,' the small man said. 'When the first one said that about wasting time, the second one said they was just following the "Big Man's" orders. Then the other one said they better get to a phone and get the Big Man in from Flamingo quick. And the second one said they oughta start down the list right off, but the first one said no they better wait.'

I did not have to guess who the Big Man was. But it gave me a hope.

'Give me the list,' I said.

I did not know if Jo-Jo was even one of the programme boys at all, but it was all I had to go on. At least, it seemed to be all Roth's boys had to go on, too. They had done me one favour anyway—they had covered the motorcycle track out in Flamingo and had probably checked out all the hotels and flops in town, with negative results. From what the small man said, it seemed like the two hoods had been in Spanish Beach before me. How? Maybe they had got Anna's letter, too, but I did not think so. They had not come to the speedway first. I remembered that Magda Olsen had not been able to get in touch with Roth, and that my two shadows had not tailed me last night. It looked very much like they had learned about Spanish Beach last night before I did. Only they had learned less than I had from Anna's letter, and something had sent them out to Flamingo. Whatever had done that I didn't know, but it gave me a chance.

'Here you go,' the small man said.

The list he gave me contained only eight names.

'I gave the other guys ten, only the picture you got rules out two of them,' the man said.

It gave me another edge. Yes it did!

They had almost an hour's start. It wouldn't do Jo-Jo much good if I got to him second. It wouldn't do me any good if it was a dead heat. If they got there first there would be some hope, because Jo-Jo would probably be on the alert. Maybe he could hold out or get away. But it was not something I could count on. No matter how I sliced it, I had to reach Jo-Jo before the two hoods. From the rest of what the small man had told me about the conversation of the two hoods, I might have a chance if they waited too long. If one of the names was really Jo-Jo at all.

'Thanks,' I said to the small man.

The man only shrugged again. He went back to his work and I went out into the Florida sun. I found a shady place, sat down, lighted a cigarette, and began to study that list of names. It wasn't going to do me any good to just start running. If the first name the two hoods checked was Jo-Jo, he was probably dead already. Or he had run again, and I'd have to go back and start over. If the two hoods were working from the wrong end of the list, that wouldn't do me any good either unless I knew which end they had started from, and that I couldn't know. No, if I just started out from one end of the list or the other, it was pure chance who found him first. What I needed was a short cut. I needed a good, gold-plated hunch that would take me right to Jo-Jo the first time.

I read the list aloud: Diego Juarez, George Hanner, Max Jones, Ted John, Andy Di Sica, Dan Black, Mario Tucci, Tom Addams. It was a nice list. It touched almost all bases. It could have been the United Nations or an East New York street gang. I smoked and laid the list in my lap and stared out into the blue space of Florida.

An alias is an interesting thing. The experts will tell you that a man can't think up an alias that won't give him away if you know enough about him. A man, they say, can't have something inside his head that did not start somewhere in his life. The alias will point to some part of his life if you just know enough about his life. Sometimes you have to know a lot about him, and sometimes very little. That depends on how smart he is, or how worried. Most small-time crooks will take aliases that are so simple anyone can spot them—usually just another variation of the real name, or one with at least the same initials. Nick-names are the same. If your name happens to be Bonnaro and you work around the docks or have maybe a big nose, you become 'Bananas'. Or if your name is Tucci, and you're dark and maybe have a black moustache, you become The Turk. Those are easy, but the experts say that if you know enough you can spot an alias every time. No man can invent an alias that is not connected to his life at some point.

I believed this. I just hoped the experts were right, and that I knew enough about Jo-Jo. I went down that list one name at a time.

Diego Juarez. It rang no bell, and it was too unusual. The small man had given me a list of tall, Nordic boys. If a boy had the name of Diego Juarez and he was tall and Nordic, it had to be his real name, or it was his appearance that had been changed, not his name.

Max Jones and Ted John were out. They did not connect in my mind, and they were too common, they sounded phony. Jo-Jo was a bright boy.

Andy Di Sica and Mario Tucci were both possibilities. There are a lot of Italians in Chelsea, and in the rackets where Jo-Jo had grown up. And Jo-Jo dreamed of the name Ferrari. Jo-Jo thought a lot of Italy. They were possibles.

Tom Addams? I didn't believe it. I heard no connection.

George Hanner. It was a good chance. It had the ring of a nice ordinary name, but one that no one had ever had. It sounded like some writer had made it up. And *Hanner* had a vague sound like *Honda*—the name of a motorcycle! I looked for quite a time at George Hanner. Then I looked at Dan Black. The bell rang. The bell clanged like an alarm. Dan Black. Nice, common, and simple, and it rang the big bell. I remembered about the Vikings. Jenny Rukowski had told me about Jo-Jo and the Vikings. Cecil Rhys-Smith had talked about Jo-Jo and the Vikings. Jo-Jo was obsessed by the Vikings. Jo-Jo knew all about them. He knew about their famous kings. I heard the list of names that Rhys-Smith had rolled off his tongue for me. The great Vikings. And one had been Halfdan the Black! You see? Halfdan the Black? Dan Black?

Was I right? How could I know until I tried? I had to make a start somewhere. I needed some luck. Don't smile. No. *Luck;* I don't care what you call it, how you explain it, how you think it operates psychologically. It is part of life. So many cases I've had, so many things in life, turn on luck, fortune, chance, accident, circumstances beyond your control. Unless you believe in some force that watches over us all and determines what will happen to us. An unseen force that can, after all, be called luck as well as anything else. I needed luck that my hunch was right about Dan Black. I needed luck that the others had not reached Dan Black yet. I would need luck to go against the two shadows, amateurs or not; aware that I was around or not. I needed luck that I would find Dan Black, alias, hopefully, Jo-Jo Olsen, at home when I got there.

I had been in a taxi all the time I was thinking about the luck I needed. I got some luck right away—the driver took me only about five blocks to a shabby motel. It was the address of Dan Black. A very cheap motel, and that was promising. An obscure transient motel, where the cabins were really shacks and the john was outside in a big central building with the showers. The driveway and courtyard were dirt. It was set back off the road, and it did not look like many cars stopped there.

I had my next luck—Dan Black was at home. The manager, a fat man uninterested in Dan Black or me or anything but the heat and his beer, said that Black was in Cabin Three. I went to Cabin Three. I was wary. It was the next to the last cabin in the row away from the road. The luck continued. There was no cover in front of the cabin and no one in sight. I circled and found no cover behind the cabin until some thick bushes about thirty feet back. Everything seemed normal. I had made it first.

That was all good luck. I got one more stroke of good luck. I knocked, and Dan Black opened the door, and I knew that I had found Jo-Jo Olsen. I felt like Stanley. I felt I had crossed Africa and Asia combined to reach him. He made no attempt to hide the fact that he was Jo-Jo Olsen.

'Hello, Jo-Jo,' I said. 'Pete Vitanza sent me. I'm Dan Fortune.'

'Yeh,' Dan Black, alias Jo-Jo Olsen, said. 'Inside. Fast!'

I stepped in. I had to step in. My good luck seemed to have run out. The big bad luck was in Jo-Jo Olsen's hand. A large .45 calibre automatic. The safety was off. Jo-Jo held it as if he knew how to use it, and it was aimed at my heart.

It had never occurred to me that Jo-Jo Olsen might not want to be rescued.

CHAPTER 17

He had darkened his hair, cut it short instead of long as it was in the picture, put on dark glasses, and half-grown, half-pasted a dark moustache. But he was Jo-Jo.

'I came down to help,' I said.

His clothes were cheap and new, but clean. Work clothes. There was a bright look to his eyes, and his voice was deep and pleasant. His hands did not shake on the automatic. There was a second pistol on his bureau. But his eyes were not hard, they were only determined.

'Who asked you to help, Fortune?' he asked quietly. 'Who asked Petey? I told him to forget it.'

I did not answer because I had no answer. Who had asked me to butt in? Who had ever asked Jo-Jo what he wanted?

'How'd you find me so easy?' Jo-Jo said.

'Who said it was easy?' I said.

He was seated on the single brass bed in that shabby room. I was in a broken-down wicker armchair. There was only the one room with two windows in the front wall and one window in the back wall, a curtained cooking area, and two shallow closets. The walls were paper thin. I could hear every sound in the next cabins and outside. I listened. Roth's men could not be far behind me. It all depended on which end of the list they had started with.

'My friend Pete,' Jo-Jo said. 'That's how you found me.'

172

'Your sister told me,' I said. 'She cares about you.'

'Who asked her?'

'They beat up Pete and killed old Schmidt,' I said.

'Pete? Schmidt?' The automatic wavered. 'Old Schmidt?'

'They killed him trying to find you.'

The automatic steadied. 'How do I know that, Fortune?'

'Schmidt's dead. Can you think of a reason? Pete's in the hospital. Look at my face.'

'A lot of guys're dead. How do I know who killed Schmidt, or beat you and Pete?'

'I know who beat me,' I said, 'I know Jake Roth when I see him. I've got a hunch we'll both be seeing him pretty soon.'

'You're a liar. You're working for the cops.'

The way he said, 'You're working for the cops.' It was not the sound of the Jo-Jo Olsen I had come to know. Maybe, under pressure, we all revert to what is easy, to what we have rejected in our lives. The way a gentle man will often become the most violent when violence is forced on him. As if the thing rejected has been lurking all the time and waiting for its chance to burst out when our painfully constructed rational defences are down. Jo-Jo was being a hard boy. Tough and cold and bitter. I didn't blame him much, but I had to reach him.

'Maybe I've got the wrong Jo-Jo Olsen,' I said. 'My Olsen had ambitions, plans. Look at you. Hiding out like any punk. Working for Jake Roth. Sure, that's what it adds up to, kid. Unless you're trying to save your own skin.'

'You want me to cry now or later?'

'Maybe you killed Nancy Driscoll after all,' I said, pushed. 'Was that the first step on the way down? No, the second step. The first step was doing a rabbit to help Jake Roth.'

'Nancy?'

It had hit him. The automatic wavered again. I pressed him.

'Tell me you didn't know?'

He blinked those bright blue eyes. 'Nancy? Dead?'

'Okay,' I said. 'Maybe they killed her, too. Roth and his boys killed her trying to find you. How many more do you want?'

The automatic shook this time. 'Nancy? What could she know about me? I didn't see her for a hell of a time. She wanted to get married.'

'When did you leave New York?' I snapped.

'Friday!'

'Can you prove it?'

'Sure I can prove it! Friday early, right after I talked to Pete. He must have told you!'

'Pete didn't see you leave the city,' I said.

'I left! Friday morn . . .' he stopped. The automatic steadied. 'You're making it up. Trying to shake me.'

'Shake you?' I said. 'You're damned right I'm trying to shake you. I've got Jake Roth after me, too. A man who was dumb enough to play with Andy Pappas' girl friend and animal enough to kill her. Who knows why? She probably knew something about him, something he didn't want Pappas to know. Sure, what else? He makes a play for a girl, makes love to her, and maybe along the way she finds out something about him he doesn't want her to tell Pappas. He gets scared. When Roth is scared he kills to shut you up. He's scared of you, kid.'

Jo-Jo said nothing. He sat on the bed and watched me. I guess he was thinking about what to do about me. Maybe if he saw I knew the whole story he'd break down. At least I hoped that was what he would do. Hope was about all I had.

'He needs that ticket, kid,' I said. 'You and me and maybe ninety-nine per cent of everyone else would have let it ride. The chances of it getting to Pappas were pretty slim. But Roth takes no chances, not when he can be safe with a little violence. I figure he killed Tani Jones just to be safe. He killed Schmidt and probably Nancy Driscoll just to find you. He mugged a cop for the other part of the ticket. You think he's going to let you live now, no matter what your father says?'

I lighted a cigarette. I had led him to where I wanted him. I wanted him to think about Swede. I wanted him to think about why he was in this mess. I smoked and waited and listened for the sounds from outside I knew had to come. It was probably a few seconds, the wait, but it seemed like an hour to me.

Then he started. 'He said Roth would feel safe, but I better take a trip anyhow. I remember the way he said it.' In that hot motel room he was seeing the scene in his home that sudden morning. Swede scared and sweating. Roth was their cousin, their way of life, and would find out anyway. 'It would be okay when I gave Mr Roth the ticket, but I better beat it anyway until it all blew over. Sure. He was on the phone telling Roth when I left.'

'He knew Roth wouldn't trust you. Not even if you gave up the ticket,' I said. 'Swede made excuses, but he knew.'

'No, he didn't know. He trusts Roth.'

'He knows now Roth has killed to find you,' I said.

'All I got to do is stay away,' Jo-Jo said.

'Roth would kill his mother to be safe,' I said. 'He killed Tani Jones to be safe.'

'I won't talk,' Jo-Jo said. 'He knows that.'

'No,' I said. 'Roth doesn't know that, kid.'

Like Swede, he was talking to himself. Only in Jo-Jo's case there was a difference. He wasn't really trying to convince himself that Roth would let him go. He was telling himself that it did not matter, that he had no choice, that this was the way it had to be. He was not thinking of himself.

'Why not talk?' I said. 'Then you'd really be safe. The police would protect you. Pappas would protect you. Talk and Roth is through.'

I'm safe anyway,' Jo-Jo said.

'Maybe,' I said, 'but why risk it? To protect Jake Roth?'

'I don't rat,' Jo-Jo said.

On his lips it sounded dirty. The sordid code of bandits and killers. There is nothing good in that dirty code of the criminal. A mean code designed to protect only sharks and parasites.

'Silence. Never talk,' I said. 'But not for Roth. It's not for Jake Roth, is it? No, silence for your family, right? That's it, and it's no good, boy. In the long run, it's no good.'

Jo-Jo looked at me. 'I owe them that.'

'You owe them,' I said, 'but not that.'

'The old man can't go back on the docks.'

'What do you owe yourself?' I said.

'I'll make out.'

'You don't really believe that they didn't know what Roth would do,' I said.

'They trust him. They believe him.'

'They don't trust him, and you don't. You're on your own against a killer, boy, and you know it.'

'No,' he said.

But his voice was down to a whisper now. I had pushed him hard. Now I played my trump.

'Why did you keep the ticket then, kid?'

Those blue eyes blinked at me. 'What?'

'You never gave Roth the ticket, did you?' I said. 'You left while Swede was on the telephone to Roth. You knew that Swede knew you had to run. When he told you it would be okay, but you better leave town anyway. You knew Roth would kill you even if you gave up the ticket. So you kept it for insurance.'

I watched him. It had figured all along that Roth did not have the ticket. Jo-Jo sat there and stared at me.

'All right,' he said. 'I never trusted him. So what?'

'They tossed you to the wolves, boy, and they did it for themselves. You know that, or you wouldn't have run with the ticket.'

'I owe them,' he said. 'They got to live. The family.'

He was really a good kid. A kid with big dreams. And he was caught. It's always harder for the good ones. He wanted no part of Swede's world. He knew what his family was, and he hated them; but he loved them, too. Whatever they were, they were his family, and he had a code of his own he was strong enough to try to stick to no matter what the risk. He might have been able to keep his code and also stay alive if I had not come along muddying the waters. I think Roth would have tried to silence him all the way anyway, but I had made it certain. It was up to me to try to save him.

'How much do you owe them, Jo-Jo?' I said. 'How much do you owe yourself?'

'I'll keep ahead,' Jo-Jo said.

'All right,' I said, 'let's say you can keep ahead of them. Let's say no one rats on you. What then, kid? What about all that you want to do? What about those big plans?'

'I'll do it all, Fortune.'

'A race driver?' I said. 'Out in the public eye? Maybe your picture in the newspaper? Who are you kidding?'

'I'll make it,' he said. But the gun shook in his hand.

'You'll make nothing! You'll be nothing,' I said, making it as harsh as I could make it. 'You won't have any experience record. You won't have any diploma or proof of education. You won't be Jo-Jo Olsen anymore. Dan Black's got no record, no history, no past and no future. You won't even be Dan Black for long. You'll never be anyone. Just a man without a name who jumps at every shadow.'

He was looking at the floor now. The automatic was down. I did not let up. I could be talking for my own life as well as his. If I did not convince him, and soon, there was no telling what he would do when Roth's men showed up. I poured it on.

'You've got three choices, kid. You can come back with me, hand that ticket over to the police, and let Roth take what's coming to him. Then you can go ahead and live your own life.

'Or you can try to keep a jump ahead of Roth. Maybe you'd make it. You'll live in shacks like this. You'll hop from town to town taking lousy jobs just to eat. You'll change your name so often you'll begin to forget who you are.

'Or you could try to talk to Roth and join him. Maybe you could convince him that you're okay, that you want to play his side of the street. I doubt if he'd believe you now, but he just might. You could even kill me for openers to show Roth how regular you are.'

That was a shocker to make him face the life it would be with Roth. Actually, I doubted that Roth would trust him now no matter what he did. It would always be too easy for Jo-Jo to get in good with Pappas by telling on Roth. Jo-Jo was ahead of me.

'There's a fourth way, Fortune,' Jo-Jo said. 'I could take the ticket to Pappas. That should put me in good. The family, too.'

I nodded. 'Why not? Only that would be the same as going in with Roth. I'm not even sure Andy would trust you now, or help your family after they tried to hold out on him, but maybe he would. Then you'd be just another punk kid hood who sooner or later would end up on a slab or in the river.'

Jo-Jo said nothing. I watched him. I blew a cloud of smoke. Now I had to try to use him against himself. I had to use who and what I knew he was.

'Besides,' I said. I leaned towards him. 'You could have done that from the start. You could have gone to Pappas in the first place. Only you couldn't do it, could you? You hate Pappas and all he stands for. You want no part of the rackets. That was why you ran in the first place. You didn't want to hurt your family by going to the police, but you couldn't stomach either covering for Roth or going to Pappas. So all you could do was run and hide.'

He sat silent. I had not told him anything he had not told himself. He was a smart kid and a good kid, and he had had a week to think all alone. I just made him face what he knew. Like a psychiatrist. He hated his father's way of life. He hated what his father had become. He hated Roth and Pappas and all that he had grown up with. He wanted to be free to do what he dreamed of doing. Yet he loved his father and the whole crummy family.

'Listen to me, Jo-Jo,' I said. 'I'm going to tell you a story. There was a kid once a lot like you. He . . . no, to hell with that. The kid was me, Dan Fortune. I was sixteen, born and raised in Chelsea. A kid no better than any other in Chelsea. It was the Depression, and it was bad. My father was a cop. Yeh, that's right. He was a cop about as good as any other. If he got a little offer of graft, maybe he took it and maybe he didn't, it depended. Maybe he was fair to people, and maybe he wasn't. My mother was a dancer and a beauty. She was alone a lot. One day my old man caught her with a guy and he nearly killed the guy. He was tossed off the force for that. He started to drink. He beat my mother regular. Then one day he left. He never could forgive her, so he left. After that she had to raise me the best she could. She got old, she wasn't so pretty, she took to booze herself. What could she do to support me? She liked men. So she had a lot of "friends," many of them on the police force. I had a different "uncle" every couple of months, and a lot of distant cousins in between.'

I stubbed out my cigarette in the seashell this cheap motel called an ashtray. My arm hurt; the missing arm. The arm that wasn't there ached from my toes to my teeth. I rubbed at it, but I knew that the ache was not going to go away. Not yet. I heard my own teeth grind in my mouth. This was the full story, the real story I never thought about and made up the other stories to hide. Now I was telling it. To save a good kid, and myself.

'I hated them. My dirty rotten father who didn't love enough to forgive or even understand. My whore of a mother who could not face life sober or alone. She couldn't face an empty bed when it got dark. Sure, she told herself that it was all for me, but it wasn't for me. She just had to have men to tell her that she was a woman even if her man had run out on her. So I hated them, and because I hated them I was going to show them I could do for them what they never did for me. I was going to take care of my mother. I was going to be a big man and show my rotten coward of a father. You know what a kid does in Chelsea if he wants to be big. Sure. He steals, he mugs, he becomes a crook.'

I lighted a cigarette. Another. My arm throbbed and my teeth hurt down to the roots. 'You do what your society tells you to do to get ahead. If I'd been born in the suburbs I'd probably have quit school to get a job and to hell with any fine future. But I was born in the slums, so I started stealing. I was pretty good. I supported my mother for a year. Then I fell into the hold of a ship I was looting. The cops couldn't touch me, but I lost my arm from that fall. In the hospital I was bitter at first, then I started to think. One night around 4 a.m. I suddenly got the message. Who was I to set myself up as judge and jury? Because that was what I was doing. My mother and father had lived their own lives, made their own choices. They were what they were. Who the hell was I to sacrifice myself for them? Who gave me the right to be responsible for their lives? I lost my arm stealing for them! I had gone out and done what my world told me to do. It had cost me my arm. And for what? I had no right to judge them, to be a martyr for them. I didn't want to be a thief. I suddenly asked myself what I wanted? *Me*. What did I owe myself?'

I smoked easier. My arm did not ache as much. 'I asked myself what I was doing? I was living their lives. I had no right to apologize for their lives. I had, somewhere, a life of my own. I had a duty to myself. My mother had to live her own life, and my father had to make his own amends. I had no right to suffer for them. When I got out of the hospital I left the city. I never broke the law again. I made my own life, Jo-Jo. Maybe I didn't make it much, but that's another story. At least I failed in my own life, not in their life.'

My throat was dry. It had been a long speech. Maybe I should have heard it more often myself and made more of my life. Who knows? All I knew is that I wanted Jo-Jo to hear it. He was young, and I had never had a son.

'People say that a good man faces his obligations,' I said. 'Maybe it's true. Only too many men face every obligation except the hard one. The hard duty is what you owe yourself. When you face your obligations to everyone else the only person you can hurt is yourself. For most people that's easy. It's a lot harder to hurt someone else, someone you love, are close to. When you hurt someone for a purpose you take the risk that the purpose wasn't worth it. Because you have to hurt them before you know you can do what you hurt them to do. You might not be worth another person's pain. You don't know until you do it, and if you fail, it's too late. It's easier to let it slide, hurt yourself for the sake of others, and feel good and noble and loved. It's harder to follow your own dream the way the old Vikings did.'

The cabin was quiet. I listened to the cars pass on the highway. Then Jo-Jo smiled. Not a smile of happiness or of triumph or of relief. A smile of simple recognition.

'They did, didn't they?' Jo-Jo said. 'The Vikings didn't take handouts. My father even lets them call him Swede.'

'It's his life, Jo-Jo,' I said.

'Yeh,' Jo-Jo said.

'Win or lose, they have their own lives,' I said. 'They made their choice. You can't live for them. The Vikings left their kids and old folks behind. Not because they were mean or cruel, but because they were honest; and it had to be that way.'

'I guess it does,' Jo-Jo said.

And that was all.

I called the police. Gazzo had been in touch, and they said they would start right out.

I borrowed Jo-Jo's extra pistol, and together we waited for the two hard boys. With any luck the police would arrive first.

We didn't have that luck.

CHAPTER 18

They came in a hired grey car, and they walked right up to the door of Cabin Three.

Why not? They expected to find only one unsuspecting boy who had never been known to carry a weapon. One scared boy on the run, supposedly even hiding out as a kind of favour to Roth, that was what they expected. I could almost see the smiles of secret anticipation on their faces as they thought about the surprise they were going to hand Jo-Jo.

I watched them get out of the car and check their guns before they came on. They put the guns loose in their suit-coat pockets and walked across the dusty courtyard to the door of Cabin Three. I went and started the water running in the sink. They knocked as easy as two men calling on a pal. We waited. They knocked again. Louder to sound above the running water.

'It's open,' Jo-Jo called out. 'Come on in.'

They stepped inside. They were that stupid. No, not stupid, arrogant. They had the arrogance of the man with the gun who has used the gun with success and not been stopped. They had that false security that comes to all dull men who have guns and think that having the gun makes them strong and bright. They were also young and inexperienced, and they had been unopposed so far; and they were near the end of the trail and already thinking of their reward.

I was behind the door when it opened. Jo-Jo was flat against the wall on the other side of the door, hidden by a kind of hat rack on legs.

The two men came in fast. They were past both of us before they saw the water running in an empty sink and started to turn to look around.

I hit the smaller one with the barrel of my borrowed gun before he turned an inch.

Jo-Jo had to hit the one with muscles three times before he went down to stay.

Neither of them got their guns out of their pockets. Jo-Jo bent to get the guns. I jumped to close the door.

The two shots hit the door frame just over my head.

Wood splinters kicked. The bullets whined away. There was blood on my face where a splinter had cut me so fast I did not feel it. I went down and inside the room, flat and backward. I hit my head a solid bump. My feet kicked the door closed. Jo-Jo headed for a window. I staggered up, a little groggy from the bump on my skull.

'No!' I shouted to Jo-Jo. 'Below the window! Stay down.'

I went to the other window. I crouched low and peered out at the lower left-hand corner. I saw their grey car, and a kind of shadow behind it. There was a bright sun. Cars were passing on the road as jaunty as you please. The flowers and trees were myriad colours. The whole scene was as ridiculous as a battlefield in any war. Even the birds were singing.

The shadow behind the car stood up warily and still half hidden. A tall, thin shadow in a grey suit.

'Roth,' I said, as much to myself as to Jo-Jo crouched at the other window. 'Watch the first two.'

Jo-Jo sat with his back to the wall and covered the two unconscious men. It was now clear why they had been so slow.

They had waited for Jake Roth. They had called Roth, as the small man at the speedway had overheard them say, and Roth had told them to wait for him before they went out after Jo-Jo. It is amazing how many mistakes a smart man can make. Of course, Jake was smart only if you mean shrewd or cunning. He was not bright, and he was both too arrogant and too careful. He made his men wait, probably to make sure himself that they really got Jo-Jo and the ticket. That had cost him his last chance.

'Listen, Jake,' I called out.

I had just heard the first faint police sirens. Roth stood out in the clear. He held a revolver.

'It's over, Jake,' I called out.

'I'll get you, Fortune,' Roth said.

He was standing there to draw a shot. I did not fall for the invitation. It would expose me, and Jake Roth was a crack shot.

'No you won't,' I said. 'Not now, and not later. We've got your two boys, and they'll talk. Olsen's got the ticket safe. We won't show ourselves. Run, Jake.'

Roth stood there. He seemed undecided. If I could keep him talking, maybe the police would arrive in time. I was not sure that that would be a favour to the cops. Roth would get someone.

'All you had to do was sit tight, Jake,' I called out into that bright sunlight. 'It was a thousand-to-one against Andy finding out. You blew it, Jake. You panicked.'

Roth said nothing. I could see the cords of his jaw muscles. He was trying to decide if he could rush us. He was still hoping we would expose ourselves. A man like Roth always thinks he will somehow handle it all and come out smelling sweet. Maybe he hoped we would fail to watch his two boys inside with us or get careless some other way.

'All you had to do was trust Jo-Jo, leave him alone,' I called out to Roth. 'You had to be sure. Just like the girl, right? You couldn't trust her either, right? Did she know something? Did she say she'd tell Andy? Did she scare you, Jake?'

But I knew the answer, of course. Fear. The answer to all of it in the end. Roth had lived so long by the gun and fear that he could only act one way. He was too afraid of Pappas. He had to be sure. A violent animal who could think of only one way to be safe—to kill anyone who could harm him. The twisted mind. The mind of all killers. They kill to be safe from some danger that, in the end, was not half as dangerous as a murder charge. They kill and complicate the simple and so defeat themselves.

'I'll get you, Fortune,' Roth said, out there in the sun. 'I'll get you, and the kid. Just like I got the others. You're dead!'

The sirens were close. It was his parting shot. It did not worry me. Roth was going to be too busy to come for me or Jo-Jo. But he had scared me, and he had beaten me, and I'm human. I could not resist a parting word.

'Run, Jake,' I called out into the sunny open space. 'Run fast, Jake.'

I saw Jo-Jo move. He was raising up to take a shot at Roth as the skinny killer got into the grey car.

'No!' I said. 'Let him go, Jo-Jo. You couldn't hit him now anyway. He can still get us if we try. Even if you hit him, he'll get some of those cops who don't even know he's here. Let him run. There'll be a better chance.'

We watched the grey car drive out of the yard and turn north on the highway. The police arrived a few minutes later. People came out of the other cabins. They were very excited. It was all quite an event. The police took us and the two hoods, who were just scared amateurs now. We told our story in the safety of a good strong cell just in case Roth had ideas of one last-gasp attempt. Jo-Jo gave them the locker key to pick up the parking ticket from the locker where he had hidden it. Then the cops took us to the airport and we flew north with a lot of friendly guards.

Captain Gazzo welcomed us with open arms and a secure paddy wagon. At headquarters Gazzo called in Andy Pappas to identify the licence number on the ticket and to give any information Pappas could in the light of the evidence. Pappas looked at that parking ticket for a long time. Andy was as dapper as ever, but he was pale; and he came alone.

'It's my small Mercury convertible,' Pappas said. 'It was down in Jersey. Jake was alone down there. You say Jake used it the day Tani . . . was killed?'

'He got it back before you returned from Washington,' Gazzo said. The captain was trying to be civil to Pappas. It was not easy for him. 'Fortune's got the whole story.'

I told Andy the story as I knew it. His face darkened when I got to the part about the Olsens. His cold eyes looked at Jo-Jo. When I told him about Roth working me over, he nodded.

'I never ordered that,' Pappas said.

'We found a losing stub from Monmouth in her place,' Gazzo said.

'Yeh,' Pappas said slowly. 'Jake was at Monmouth the day before. I remember.'

'His two hired hands are singing anyway,' Gazzo said. 'The whole story, as much as they know of it.'

'Yeh,' Pappas said. He stared at the parking ticket. He licked his dry lips. 'Do you know what . . . I mean, what happened? In her place?'

'You mean why did he kill her?' I said. 'His two boys say that he told her some big plan he had. He shot his mouth off, that's the way the two hoods put it, and then he had to cool her.'

'Plans?' Pappas said, his dead eyes narrowed to slits.

'Plans against you, Pappas,' Gazzo said. 'It looks like Jake was making a play for Tani, and to show her what a big man he was he told her some plans he had.'

'He didn't go to kill her,' I said. 'He went to play games with her. But he made a mistake, and he had to silence her.'

'Jake and Tani?' Pappas said. 'Yeh. She was just a poor dumb kid who liked men. I guess she just had to play around. But you know something? The kid loved me. Yeh, she did.'

'I know,' I said. 'That's what killed her.'

I could picture the scene that afternoon. Jake Roth, alone with Tani, encouraged by her, and for one arrogant instant sure that she would prefer him to Pappas. After all, he was younger, and in his own mind a better man. He was sure she would choose him, but with a faint doubt, a small need to impress. So he told her of some plans, his big schemes. Probably a boast that he would soon be the boss. Then, a moment later, aware of his error. Maybe he saw it in her eyes. The shock, the horror she was too naive to hide. In that one instant Roth must have seen the truth: that he was only a momentary little excitement to Tani, and that Pappas was the big thing, the important man to her. Maybe Tani did not know who Pappas really was, or care, but she knew a threat to her man when she heard one. Jake Roth saw that, realized his mistake, and acted in the only way Roth could act. He shot her.

'He shot her then and there, Andy,' I said, 'but you killed her. Fear of you, Andy, that's what killed Tani. She was your woman, and Jake knew he couldn't risk leaving her alive a minute.'

I clubbed him with those words, but I felt almost sorry for him then. All at once he was just another middle-aged man who had lost his sweetheart. It did not matter that he had had little right to have a sweetheart. All men need some love in their lives, and what did I know about his home life? I felt almost sorry. But only almost. Because he was not just another middle-aged man.

He was Andy Pappas, and he had some pain coming to him. So I clubbed him with words. Not that it did any good.

'You did good, Danny,' Pappas said, as if he had not heard me. 'I'll send you a cheque even if you didn't do the job for me. That kid, too. The one who was beaten up.'

'No cheque,' I said. 'Not for me. I made that choice a long time ago, Andy. What you touch dies.'

'Suit yourself,' Andy said.

'You killed her as sure as if you'd pulled that trigger yourself,' I said.

Pappas began to pull on those white gloves he affects now. He still did not hear me. He never hears or sees what he does not want to hear or see. He smoothed the fingers of the gloves. He looked at Gazzo.

'Is that all, Captain?'

'That's all,' Gazzo said. 'Unless you want to tell us what Roth thought he was going to take over.'

Pappas smiled a thin smile. He nodded to me and went out of the office. As he went I saw his hand smooth his suit coat at the place where he used to carry his gun under the coat. Gazzo saw that, too. There was a look of sudden hope in Gazzo's eyes. The captain was thinking that maybe Andy would slip this time, kill Roth himself, get caught. I doubted that. There would probably be a small purge of anyone Pappas learned had been associated with Jake Roth in his plans, but Pappas would not be personally involved. How far could true love make a man stupid?

In the interrogation room the two hoods sang like eager tenors. They told all about what Jake had done and what he had hired them to do.

'We was to get the ticket and kill Olsen. The old man was just lousy luck. We asked some questions, and he kicked off on us.

They looked at us as if it was somehow old Schmidt's fault that he had died. It was unfair to them that he had died. Anyone could see that. They seemed to think that this explanation made it all okay, that we should kiss and make up.

'Roth was gonna give us good spots when he took over,' the muscle-boy explained. 'I mean, it was our chance, you know? The big break. We'd of been right on top with the boss.'

The thin one shrugged. 'Maybe he wasn't so smart. I mean, spilling to that Jones kid was a dumb play. Yeh, real dumb.'

Jake Roth made a dumb mistake. Now people were dead.

'What about Nancy Driscoll?' I said.

The muscle boy shook his head. 'We don't know no Driscoll, like we told the cap'n. I guess Jake handled her himself, like he done with you, peeper.'

'How did you know where Olsen was?' I asked.

'Jake told us,' the thin one said. 'Only he didn't do so good about that, neither. We got down there way ahead of you, Fortune, except he had us out in that dirt town Flamingo. We turned that cycle track upside down, 'n then we looked all over Spanish Beach before Jake says to try the speedway.'

'And you have nothing to tell us about Nancy Driscoll?' Gazzo said.

'No sir, Cap'n, nothin',' the thin one said.

After we gave Gazzo all we could about Roth, Jo-Jo and I walked out into the morning. We had been at it all night. Gazzo had the manhunt underway. The day was going to be hot and stifling in the city. Jo-Jo did not seem to want to go home. I suggested he take a hotel room. I'd lend him the money even if I had to borrow it from Marty or Joe.

'Thanks, Mr Fortune,' Jo-Jo said.

He had removed his moustache by now, and taken off the dark glasses. He stood in the city morning and looked up and down the street as if not quite sure that it was all over and not quite sure of what to do next. That is one of the problems of choosing to go your own way. For a long time it seems like you have nothing much to do, because you are so accustomed to doing what other people want you to do. Jo-Jo was missing all the sense of purpose of the last week when he was running and hiding for the sake of his family.

'Only let's go and call on Petey first,' I said. 'I owe my client a report, after all.'

Jo-Jo shrugged. We caught a taxi and rode in the growing heat and glare of the morning towards St Vincent's. Jo-Jo was not talkative. I suppose he was thinking of his new life. It takes time to adjust to facing yourself, to throw off a whole set of preconceived notions.

In a way I was doing the same thing. I was thinking of Pete Vitanza, and adjusting to my thoughts.

CHAPTER 19

In the taxi I opened the window to get the air on my face.

'You sent Pete a note too, didn't you?' I said. 'When I first showed at the motel you thought that Pete had told me you were in Spanish Beach.'

Jo-Jo nodded. 'Yeh, I sent him a note. Him and Anna.'

'But you didn't mention cars or your job,' I said, 'and you probably didn't mail it right in Spanish Beach.'

'I just said the weather was fine. I figured he'd know I meant I was okay,' Jo-Jo explained. 'I guess I mailed it the night I went over to the bike races in Flamingo.'

'That was lucky,' I said.

'Lucky?' Jo-Jo said.

'Someone told Roth you were in, or near, Spanish Beach,' I said. 'He looked in Flamingo first, and then he looked around the town for a while because he figured you'd never go near the speedway. He was too damned clever for his own good.'

Jo-Jo blinked at me. 'But Pete hired you.'

'Yeh,' I said. 'He hired me'

At the hospital they did not want to let us see Pete at first. I told them that it was police business and important. The police still had a man at the door of Pete's room. The officer knew me and my connection to the case and let us go in.

Pete lay in bed. He was still weak, but the bandages were off his face. He struggled to sit up as we came in. I saw him bite his lip in pain. His face was scarred with raw wounds, and his arms were still splinted and bandaged; but he grinned to Jo-Jo.

'Hello, buddy,' Pete said. And said to me, 'Thanks, Mr Fortune.'

'I came to report to my client,' I said.

'So report,' Pete said, and winked at Jo-Jo.

I told the story. Pete listened closely. The white room was bright with the morning sun. Jo-Jo stood away from the bed. When I told Pete about the final part with the two hoodlums and Jake Roth, Pete's face seemed to darken under the scars and bruises.

'I hope they burn!' Pete said. 'Roth got away though, huh?'

'They'll get him,' I said. 'But probably not alive.'

Pete agreed. 'He won't get took alive.'

'I was lucky to get to Jo-Jo first,' I said.

'Lucky as hell for Jo-Jo,' Pete said. 'Right, buddy?'

Jo-Jo nodded from across the room. 'Real lucky, Pete.'

'Mr Fortune, he knows his job,' Pete said. 'I hired the right man, all right.'

There was a silence in the room. Pete grinned at both of us. Jo-Jo had picked up a metal water jug and was examining it. I had a good view out the window from where I stood at the bed. I could not look at the view forever.

'Why didn't you tell me about the note Jo-Jo wrote to you, Pete?' I said. 'I guess the nurse read it to you, right?'

Pete nodded. 'Yeh, I remembered soon as you left, you know? Stupid. It was when you told me about old Schmidt and talked about movin' that car. I just forgot the note, damn.'

'No,' I said, 'you didn't forget.'

Pete's eyes were like two shallow puddles with a dark film of ice on them. The bruises and scars on his face seemed to stand out. The muscles of his jaw twitched.

'Roth knew that Jo-Jo was around Spanish Beach, Pete,' I said. 'He knew before I did. Wild horses wouldn't have dragged it out of Anna, and if she had told Roth, she wouldn't then have told me.'

Pete said nothing. He looked at Jo-Jo.

'There's only one way Roth could have known about Spanish Beach, Pete,' I said.

Pete nodded. His dark eyes flickered away from Jo-Jo and from me. He looked at the wall. Then he looked back at Jo-Jo. He looked straight at Jo-Jo as if he had gathered courage.

'He came here, Roth did,' Pete said. 'He was gonna beat me again. I couldn't take any more. I'm sorry, buddy.'

'No,' I said.

Now Pete looked at me. For the first time I saw something move under the flat surface of his eyes.

'What?' Pete said. 'What?'

'He didn't beat it out of you, Pete. He didn't even try to. How could he do that here? And how would he have known Jo-Jo had written to you? No, you called him, Petey. You told him on your own. Why?'

'I don't know how he found out about the note, but he did! Okay, maybe I got too scared too easy, but if you got beat as bad . . . hell, I hired you, Mr Fortune.'

'Yeh,' I said, 'you hired me. But not to find Jo-Jo, Pete. Not to find him. It was a little strange all along. I mean, that you would come to me. You knew Jo-Jo was in trouble.'

Jo-Jo spoke. He still held the water jug. 'I told you I had trouble.'

'Sure,' Pete said, 'but you never said you was gonna run! You never said what trouble!'

'You knew I had trouble,' Jo-Jo said. 'You knew I was on the run.'

I took it up. 'By all the normal rules, Pete, you should have minded your own business, right? If Jo-Jo had trouble and you guessed it was connected to Stettin like you said, you should have been quiet as a tomb. That is, if you wanted to help Jo-Jo. But you came to me. I figure you'd even guessed about Tani Jones. I figure you even knew it was Roth after Jo-Jo all along. But you came to me even though you knew that when I started looking it would cause Jo-Jo more trouble.'

'I wanted you to find him, help him! Is that so bad? How would I know it was gonna work out bad? Hell, you did save him, didn't you? It worked out okay!'

'Sure, it worked out fine, but not for you,' I said. 'You hired me to make trouble, Pete, not to stop it.'

Pete said nothing. The hospital room was very sunny now, and hot. Jo-Jo had put down the metal water jug and was watching Pete. Pete just sat there propped up. I suppose he was still weak. Or maybe just tired. I suppose he had been thinking about all of this ever since he had heard that Jo-Jo was safe and Roth was on the run instead.

'Jo-Jo,' I said, 'where's your miniature Ferrari good-luck piece?'

'My Ferrari?' Jo-Jo said. He took out his key ring. 'Right here, why?'

I took the good-luck charm and held it up in front of Pete Vitanza. Petey just stared at it, those dark eyes as flat and opaque as mud. The charm, Jo-Jo's good-luck piece, was dull and battered and scratched as it would have to have been if carried for long in his pocket with his keys. It was exactly like the charm Gazzo had found under Nancy Driscoll's body.

'Let's see your charm again, Pete,' I said.

Pete did not move.

'Never mind,' I said. 'I remember it. It was new and shiny, Pete, wasn't it? The miniature you showed me was new. Jo-Jo, when did Petey buy his charm?' 'When I did,' Jo-Jo said.

'So I bought a new one,' Petey said. 'I lost mine, yeh.' 'Sure,' I said. 'You lost it all right.'

Pete stammered. 'There're hundreds of them! Thousands!'

'Sure there are,' I said. 'I remember something that manager, Walsh, said. He talked about Jo-Jo and Nancy, how Nancy said that all they talked about was cars and motors. Plural, Pete, you understand? More than one person talked to Nancy about cars.'

Then Jo-Jo spoke up. He had guessed what I was saying at last. That's how I had wanted it to happen.

'We used to go up to her place together sometimes.' Jo-Jo said. 'Yeh, I remember. When she came around, he talked to her. Yeh, I remember how he looked at her.'

'Damn it, everyone knows I knew her!' Pete said, cried.

'Sure, but not that way. You had a yen for her, didn't you, Pete; a big yen,' I said. 'The miniature, the grease-stained handkerchief, anything else that fits Jo-Jo fits you, too. You acted like you barely knew her. But you implied all along that she could be involved in it all. You sent me to her, Pete.'

'You knew I hadn't even seen her for months,' Jo-Jo said.

'You knew she wouldn't know anything about Jo-Jo,' I said.

'You knew I left town before she got killed,' Jo-Jo said.

'You knew no one would go to her to look for Jo-Jo,' I said.

Our voices hammered at him, beat him, slashed him.

'No! I didn't know! Those two hoods beat her. Roth got to her! Sure, that was it, Roth got to her. Roth!'

He was like a trapped animal. A small animal caged in that bed and unable to move or run or hide. He thrashed like a fish in a net. I did not like what I was doing, but I had to push him. I had to push him right to the wall.

'You brought her into it, Pete,' I said. 'You sent me to her. You wanted all of them connected to her, because you knew she was dead. You killed her, Pete, and then you remembered that Jo-Jo was on the run.'

'No!'Pete shouted. 'No!'

'She had a man with her late Saturday afternoon,' I said. 'A drunk kid. That was you. Jo-Jo was gone, you were lonely I guess; you had always wanted her. You went up there. I don't know what happened. I don't suppose you meant to kill her, you're not Jake Roth. I figure you got crazy drunk. You hit her, Pete. You hit her and hit her and hit her and hit her!'

'No,' Pete said. 'No . . . no . . .' But he was backed to the wall, and there was no power left in his voice.

'You were scared. I'd have been scared. You wiped her face. I guess you tried to revive her. You saw she was dead. That was when you ran. How far did you run, Pete? All the way back to Chelsea? Were you back here and feeling safer when you found that you had dropped that miniature Ferrari? When you saw you'd left the handkerchief, and the bottle? You were not one of her regular men, but you had left that Ferrari, and sooner or later the police would dig you out. You've seen them work. They don't give up easy, no. There was that Ferrari, right? It was the Ferrari miniature that gave you the idea, sure. Jo-Jo had one just like it. Jo-Jo was a real boyfriend. Jo-Jo was on the run. Jo-Jo was already in trouble.'

I stopped. I waited. Pete had turned his face to the wall of that white room. 'You decided to give Jo-Jo to the police. You're a bright kid. You probably even figured that someone was after Jo-

Jo, and maybe that someone would get blamed. Or maybe you'd be real lucky and Jo-Jo would never be found, not alive. A dead Jo-Jo would be a great suspect. Maybe you even knew it was Roth after him by then. Maybe, not. But you sure knew about Stettin and maybe even Tani Jones. You wanted someone blamed; you know the cops don't stop looking unless they have someone to pin a killing on; it doesn't look good. So you got the bright idea to give them Jo-Jo. You got the idea to stir it all up by hiring me to make waves. You knew I'd go to the police about Jo-Jo's rabbit act. You knew the police, or maybe me, would connect Jo-Jo to Nancy Driscoll.'

I could not see those flat, dark eyes. His head was turned away. But I saw his shoulders shake. 'I don't suppose you wanted him dead, not at first. I don't suppose you even thought about that. You just wanted a smokescreen. But then you got beaten up, and you knew there were some hard people after Jo-Jo. That was a break for you, that beating. It made you look good, and it gave you more possible killers of Nancy Driscoll. After all, she had been beaten, too. You got too smart, Pete. You sent me after Nancy, you pushed too hard. You got to thinking that it would be a lot better if the police never found Jo-Jo alive. With what they had on him, if they found him dead, they'd probably pin her killing on him and close the books. Or pin it on the same guys who killed him. It didn't matter which. If they got him alive, it would not be so good. So you called Roth and told him where to find Jo-Jo. And that was your mistake. Because only you could have told Roth. You had the letter from Jo-Jo.'

He was still weak. Maybe he was tired. In that bed he could not run or fight. And he knew what he had done. There is an urge to confess. There is, ask any cop. I'll leave the why of that to the psychiatrists, but I know it is true, I've seen it too often. I've seen a hundred men with no proof against them that will stand up in court, with just enough suspicion on them to be hauled in for questioning, and sooner or later they confess. No rubber hoses. Just weariness and perhaps guilt and that something else I can't explain—that urge to finally tell. Maybe it is only that it becomes too hard to lie when you know the truth. I'm not talking about the professional criminal, the Jake Roth. I'm talking about the ordinary man who never wanted to kill. A man like Pete Vitanza. He had not meant to kill, I was sure of that, and he was filled by guilt, but he was also afraid, and he tried once more.

'You got nothin'll stand up,' Pete said. His face towards the wall. 'You got no proof.'

'I've got enough to make Gazzo take you downtown, Pete,' I said. 'He'll ask the questions, Pete. I've got enough for that. You know how Gazzo'll ask. You know you'll tell him.'

When he turned from that wall his battered face was almost calm. His dark eyes were no longer flat. The eyes had depth again; they had colour. He had been afraid, worried, for a long time now, and it was over. His face even seemed younger under the bruises. He looked at both of us from the bed. His arms stuck out like bandaged boards.

'She turned me down.' There was a tone of surprise in his voice as if he still could not believe that Nancy Driscoll had turned him down. 'I was drunk. I mean, Jo-Jo was gone and I got drunk. So I went up to her place. I took a bottle and some beer. I was there a long time. She threw the tease at me. The bitch! I mean, she shook it all in my face. She gave me the full show. Then she said no. I mean, she said no! I hit her. She called me a pig. She called me a punk, a kid. A dirty pig she said. I hit her again. She was on the floor and I hit her some more. I hit her a lot more. I was crazy drunk. I hit her. Then she didn't move. I remember something like screams, you know? I mean, I didn't hear her scream, I just sort of remember. She stopped moving. She was on the floor. I wiped her face. She was dead.'

Pete stopped. His arms stuck straight out. His eyes saw the dead face of Nancy Driscoll. He closed his eyes.

'So you wiped the beer cans and the bottle,' I said. 'You've seen the movies. They always wipe off the fingerprints. You took the address book. Maybe your name was in it. But you ran too soon. You left too much. Later you remembered what you had left, and you remembered that Jo-Jo was on the run. Everything you'd left fitted Jo-Jo, too. It looked like a good chance for you. Just frame Jo-Jo. With any luck Jo-Jo might not even be alive to deny it—only you had to be sure Jo-Jo was tied to the Driscoll girl. That was where I came in.'

'I was scared,' Pete said. His eyes were still closed. He shivered there in the bed. 'I was so scared . . . so scared . . .'

I went to the telephone to call Gazzo.

Jo-Jo walked out of the hospital room without speaking again. Not to Pete, and not to me.

CHAPTER 20

Pete signed a statement for Captain Gazzo while he was still in the hospital. When he could get up, Gazzo took him downtown and booked him. I went back to Marty.

'Why do they confess, baby?' Marty asked. 'They always do, men like Pete.'

'I don't know,' I said. 'Maybe because they're not really killers. The killing is panic, a moment of irrationality, an emotional accident. When the moment is over they become themselves again, and the guilt and horror gets to them.'

'But he tried to get Jo-Jo killed, too.'

'That's another matter,' I said. 'That was fear. No one knew anything, and he had a chance to evade it all. Pin it on another man, that's the way we are. He might have got away with it if he hadn't tried too hard. Just like Jake Roth. All either of them had to do was sit tight and they would probably have never been caught.'

We were in her apartment. There were no more shadows waiting out in the dark, or at least no shadows I knew about. No shadows beyond the normal shadows that are always waiting. I had a beer in my hand, it was cool in the room, and Marty was there. Only a week had passed since I had brought Jo-Jo Olsen back from Florida, but it was already history, something to be talked about with a fine detachment.

'It's that word *probably*,' Marty said. 'They couldn't sit tight. They couldn't live with the danger hanging over them, maybe for the rest of their lives. To never know when it might all be discovered? Listen for every knock at the door? They chose to try to end the danger all the way. *Whether 'tis nobler in the mind to suffer the slings and arrows of outrageous fortune, Or to take arms against a sea of troubles, And by opposing end them.* I suppose I'd think that way, too. Killers are human, baby. Pete would have lived with fear every day. He tried to get away free.'

She's a good actress. Maybe she'll have a chance someday. Not to do *Hamlet,* of course. Sometimes it bothers her that there are so many parts she can't do; that she's a woman and not a man. I'm glad she's a woman. Anyway, women have done *Hamlet.* She might get the chance to even do that, you never know. Of course, she was right. That was what Pete and Jake Roth could not face even if they did not know it consciously: the threat that would always hang over them. They had to try to get clear no matter how many people had to suffer or die.

'A noble principle,' I said, 'and a rotten result. The name of the game. Par for the course. Action without ethics. I guess it's not all Pete's fault. No one ever taught him ethics.'

'What will happen to him, Dan?'

'Manslaughter,' I said. 'They could go for murder two, but they won't. He'll go away for a good trip. Maybe he'll learn something, but I doubt it. He's weak.'

'Don't be righteous, baby. Fear makes a man do a lot.'

'Even Jake Roth?'

'Even Jake Roth,' Marty said.

We all talked about it for a time. It was good conversation, but life went back to normal. The two hired punks were indicted on various counts of assault and attempted murder, and one good count of murder two. The district attorney's office could have gone for murder one on Schmidt and probably got it, but juries can be chancy, and big trials cost the state a lot of money. The two punks were not important enough to waste time or money on. They would plead guilty to the lesser counts, and that would put them away just about forever.

Jake Roth continued to run free, but he ran. Roth went on a nationwide hookup. Every cop was looking for him, not to mention Pappas and his connections. It was only a matter of time. But Roth was no amateur, and he made it a matter of a long time.

Autumn came to Chelsea and moved on towards winter. I began to get a little nervous. Roth eluded the police and Pappas. In Chelsea they began to lay odds on how long Roth could keep it up and on who would get to him first. The smart money, of course, was on Pappas and his minions. The smart money is always cynical, on the obvious and the worst of human nature, and it is usually the winner. Which says a lot about the world. A few dreamers got long odds on Jake actually making it away. There are always a few who believe in long odds and the miracle that will make them rich, and there are also always a few who see even Jake Roth as Robin Hood. That also says a lot.

Joe thought that what Roth should do was come in and surrender to the police.

'The longer he stays out, the closer Pappas gets,' Joe said behind his new bar in a good Village joint. 'They ain't got enough to make the Jones killing stick.'

'What about Schmidt?' I said.

'A good shyster could handle that,' Joe said. 'Hell, the only witnesses are those two punks. A good shyster could make the jury cry. None of it's sure to nail him.'

'It never was enough,' I said. 'But it's enough for Pappas. It was always Pappas. Out or inside it's the same. Once in a cell Roth'd be lucky to live a week. In jail he's a sitting duck. He'd be dead from the first minute, only Pappas would let him sweat, and Roth'd never know when or how it would happen. All he can do is run and never stop.'

In the end it was the police who got to Roth first. A lot of smart money was lost in Chelsea, which shows that there is maybe some hope for us all. Roth was cornered in a loft in Duluth on a cold day in November. He tried to shoot his way out. All he did was achieve a kind of suicide. He had not been able to get out of the country, he had lost twenty-five pounds, and he was all alone. They covered him with canvas, took the body to the morgue, and no one ever claimed the body. Nobody anywhere felt sorry for him.

If this was an uplifting story, I'd probably tell you that Jo-Jo Olsen's decision to accept his duty to himself worked out best for everyone. But it didn't.

In prison Pete is not taking it well. The last I heard he is bitter. He is bitter against his rotten luck. He is bitter against me. He has decided that he got a bad deal because the Driscoll girl deserved what she got—she was no good anyway. They say he is growing harder all the time up there.

With Roth gone Swede Olsen is out. Pappas is aware of what the Olsens did to cover for Jake, and word has it that the Olsens at least knew about Roth's plans to become boss instead of Pappas, if they weren't actually involved. (Which adds a dimension to their actions, they were afraid of Pappas, too. They had reason to be. Since Roth died, some other gang faces are missing from Chelsea and Little Italy, too.)

Pappas does not forgive. Sometimes, when I've been up all night, or when I can't sleep because the missing arm hurts or Marty is busy, I walk past the docks at dawn and see Swede Olsen standing there in the shape-up. He's not young, and Pappas is down on him, so he doesn't get much work even when he goes out and stands there in the dawn waiting to be picked out of the shape. He doesn't drink in the good bars anymore. He drinks in the cheapest saloons. They say he drinks a lot now.

Magda Olsen spat on Jo-Jo in Gazzo's office. As she said, she had five kids, but only one Jake Roth to make life sweet. The two Olsen boys who backed Swede are out as far as he is. One of them is with him on the docks and gets just about as much work. The other boy has left home. No one knows where he is or cares. The boy in college is back in Chelsea working as a cook in a diner. The daughter, Anna, left home, too. I see her from time to time on the street. She has a job, a decent boyfriend, and she may be okay.

Jo-Jo never went home. I don't know where he went. He never contacts me. Why should he? We hardly knew each other. I look for his name in the newspapers, maybe as a member of the Ferrari team. I don't really expect to see it, and yet I just might someday. As I said at the start, a story is not in the facts and events, but in who and what a man is, and Jo-Jo goes all the way back to the Vikings. That was what made him run in the first place instead of going to Pappas or helping Roth, and that was what brought him back in the end to finish Jake Roth and Pete Vitanza. He has the sense of what a real man must do.

'When we all have that,' Marty said, 'we'll even finish Andy Pappas.'

We were in the dark of her bedroom. It was near Christmas, and there were bright coloured lights all along the street outside; the Christmas lights and crowds all through the holiday city.

'We don't want to finish Andy Pappas,' I said.

It was a cold night. There was snow on the streets. Marty was warm and close to me.

'We don't care about Pappas as long as he doesn't touch us,' I said. 'Each of us alone. To hell with what Pappas does to the other guy.'

'Think about Jo-Jo.' Marty said.

She said it into my ear, her lips close, soft.

'I'm thinking about Pete Vitanza and Jake Roth and those two hoods and that manager Walsh and Pappas,' I said. 'I'm thinking that in the same boat as Roth how many of us would have acted any different? I'm thinking about all of them, and only one Jo-Jo.'

'If there's one, there can be more,' Marty said. 'Maybe everyone.'

'I'd like to believe it,' I said.

And I would like to believe that. I would really like to believe that Jake Roth and Pete Vitanza were really only freaks. But my judgment is against me.

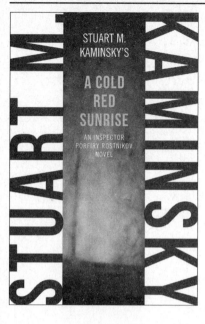